PHYLLIS THE DONKEY GIRL

AND OTHER TRUE TALES

Phyllis The Donkey Girl

... And Other True Tales

Trevor C. Trower

TAMARIND TREE
Toronto

Tamarind Tree Books Inc.,
14 Ferncastle Crescent,
Brampton, Ontario. L7A 3P2, Canada.
Or
Trevor C. Trower,
14071, Fifth Side Road,
Georgetown, Ontario. L7G 4S5, Canada

Library and Archives Canada Cataloguing in Publication

Title: Phyllis the donkey girl : ...and other true tales / Trevor C. Trower.
Names: Trower, Trevor C., 1927- author.
Description: Includes index.
Identifiers: Canadiana 20200269313 | ISBN 9781989242018 (softcover)
Subjects: LCSH: Trower, Trevor C., 1927- | LCSH: Great Britain—Anecdotes.
    | LCSH: Canada—Anecdotes.
Classification: LCC PS8639.R697 Z46 2020 | DDC C818/.609—dc23

Cover: Adapted from pictures by (Sunset) -Rene Raushchenberger/Pixabay Licence & (Airplane) Gary Lopater/Unsplash Licence

Dedication

For Victor, Grace, Brendon and Betty. With love.

CONTENTS

Contents

INTRODUCTION

As I have added years onto my aging frame, my pleasures in this life more and more became those where a degree of wit is required to compensate for the more physical activities. I love to read and hear a good story as you might surmise from the content in this book.

I have a fondness for recording my history in writing.

A publisher once informed me and others in my group, that there are only two types of writers:
- One instructs
- The other entertains

I hope you find the anecdotes I've described herein to be entertaining. It certainly gave me a lot of pleasure writing the stories.

Trevor C. Trower,
Toronto, 2020.

Goodbye Plymouth, Hello Rhyl -1941

The day we were forced to leave Plymouth the local newspaper headline read "Plymouth Suffers 420th air-raid of the war," it was April, 1941. Our family consisted of my soldier father, my mother with a month-old baby named Judy and seven other children, aged two to eighteen years. I had just turned fourteen at that time and I can only see the move from Plymouth from my own perspective and memory. My earliest recollection of my Plymouth happened to take place at our home in Sydney Terrace, in downtown Plymouth.

I was four years old. Daily, I walked with my older sister Grace, who was six, to our public school at the end of our street and around the corner. School was not a baby-sitting service for small children. We were taught the three "R's," and though I can't recall the details, I can certainly tell you that by the age of six we all could read and write quite well. Later, I remember that my Mother would show off my younger brother Glyn's ability, when at five he could read from the newspaper. I vividly recall the delight of my parents whenever Glyn would demonstrate this skill.

My first teacher was a wonderful person who was an expert motivator. There was one incident which took place during my first year at school, the teacher asked the class "How many ten-shilling notes are there in a pound note?"

No-one replied. The class was comprised of nearly forty children, all of about the same age. The teacher repeated the question and again there was no reply.

"Trevor," she called, and with a smile said "Can you tell us how many ten shilling notes there are in a pound?"

"Two, Miss," I shyly replied.

My correct answer elicited a sweet reward. The teacher, standing in front of the class, bent over and lifted the hem of her skirt, which came to her ankles, she gathered the skirt in her hand and lifted it above her knees. An inch or so above her right drawer's leg was a little pocket with a small, appliquéd butterfly. She inserted her finger and thumb and pulled out a small, shallow, cardboard box about the size of a matchbox with the Name "IMPS" imprinted on it, she withdrew a tiny, black, licorice, candy from the package and I received my reward. This was the way Miss would reward her charges whenever a child would show particular cleverness, how delicious.

The Sydney Terrace house, where we all lived in the basement, was an older home and quite run down. Three working class families lived there sharing the space with the usual bugs and mice. At that time, our family comprised of Mother, Father and four kids, Victor, Grace, baby Glyn and me. Victor and Grace were allowed to go out to play but I was kept inside. Mind you I was able to climb onto the kitchen table and look out the window and watch them at their play.

On one occasion from that position I watched as an elongated, balloon-like structure floated across the blue-grey sky. I clearly remember its markings, written across its huge, grey, bloated, side was its name "R-100," it was a famous airship.

We vacated the Sydney Terrace house and after several moves we settled in a council- house, #8, Laurel Dene, Swilly. This was quite luxurious as compared to our earlier home. We now had three bedrooms and a large back yard. My Father had not only been a soldier but also a newspaper subscription salesman, an ocean-liner steward, waiter and a civilian employee at the seaplane base "Mountbatten," but for much of the time he was unemployed like millions of others. Drinking bouts kept the family in abject poverty. It was the bitter arguments and horrible abuse which caused the most pain. On one occasion we thought our Mother would be killed, it didn't seem possible that the quiet man of the day could possibly be the same person as that earlier cruel and angry, drunken, man.

As a lad I spent many happy, hours, fishing at or near the Barbicain. Like most poor boys I'd scrounge string from parcels and cases and use a hook only as we lacked bait. I'd look for discarded cigarette packets to use the foil to wrap around the hook then add a few inches of red, wool wrapped around the lure. Sometimes the pollack would fall for the trap and we would have fish for supper. I remember the exciting smell of the Barbicain, a mixture of salt air, fish and at low tide there was the black, slimy, mud. I'd shout "Hello" to the men on the small fishing boats as they entered the harbor, I always gave a wave and a cheery greeting, and sometimes a surplus cod or pollack was provided from those kind and generous men. Plymouth. What a magnificent city, steeped in history and in those days, shared by perhaps a quarter of a million people.

As a junior schooler, I had been fairly successful, a bright but messy student. I was a happy little boy and always tried to please my teachers, however, for whatever reason I was not always able to do so. I remember well our headmaster at our North Prospect Public School, a short, fat, grey-suited little man with wet, red lips. He would visit our class occasionally and select the cutest little girl and sit her on his knee as he asked her to repeat her lesson. He would smile into the little girl's face and say "Well done." I recall the dreadful caning he would also deal out. He seemed to really enjoy caning us boys.

There was one occasion, like an unexpected holiday or jam for tea that brought us great joy. Mr. Sloggett our Geography teacher, sent Alwyn, a plump, pretty boy to the principal for not paying attention to the lesson. While the headmaster was caning him he suddenly broke away and escaped. The class continued for a while, then we could see Alwyn and his mother striding down the corridor to the head's office. She burst into the office and began to punish Mr. Palmer for caning her boy. First with curses then she picked up his cane and began to lash him with it. Palmer ran screaming from his office and hid in the janitor's room until the excitement died down. I don't remember seeing Alwyn after that, I think he was enrolled into another school.

The cane and other forms of cruel punishment left a lasting impression on me. I was sent to the Head's office once. I remember plucking hairs from my head to put on my hands to prevent pain. The trick didn't work. The pain was so awful I didn't feel the additional pain as he lashed me across my back while leaving his office to go back to class. I was ten years old then and I have always felt that many who become leaders, that is supervisors, foremen, NCO's, and so on, often exhibit traits that should preclude them from being in charge of others.

It appeared that my transition from public school to High School was not too satisfying. Following the summer of '38 I entered High School, Plymouth Public Cobourg Street High. What a marvelous institution. To put all students on an equal basis as far as class was concerned, school uniforms were mandatory. Grey flannels, a green blazer piped with yellow trim and a schoolboy's cap. The breast pocket and cap were adorned with the school emblem the Oak Tree, symbolizing strength and honor.

The student body was divided into four sections of equal number and were known as "Houses." The groups were known as - Roots, Leaves, Acorns and Branches. I was a Leaf, and I always tried to justify my pride in being of that fraternity. It was difficult being on sports teams as certain items of equipment had to be provided by the parents, which meant that I could not play soccer, rugby or cricket, we had no money for regular wear. I was provided with shoes or rather boots from our church. To prevent my footwear ending up traded for alcohol for my father, three holes were punched in the ankle area of each boot to identify it as welfare. I distinctly remember my black cleated boots versus the other boys brown shoes. Mind you once I started to wear long pants it was not too bad.

I was in 2B when the war started and I continually found schoolwork a real chore. I rarely did home-work and once the war started there were lots of reasons preventing me from doing my best. When the war broke out my father joined the army and my mother received a small weekly family allowance, this was the first time in years we had actual and regular cash.

My older brother was in a sanatorium, my older sister worked in a market garden which meant we lived relatively comfortable in our house in Swilly. Most men had joined the military and many women served in the WAAFS, WRENS etc. men and women who had not joined the forces served as air-raid wardens, volunteer fire-fighters, first-aid workers and so on. In many instances the war brought out the best in local citizens and those were recognized for their tireless efforts and exploits and were rewarded with medals, titles and other awards.

Shortly after his release from Didworthy Sanatorium, my older brother presented himself to the army recruitment centre, his examination revealed evidence of lung scaring though the TB was no longer active. He was declared unfit for military service. He became an apprentice at the Royal Naval Dockyard. I understand his duties were two-fold, first, making tea for the men, and second, keeping watch for the foreman while the men played cards. Later, Victor joined the Home Guards. I learned a lot from my brother, probably the most interesting being how to make use of the Carbide which he worked with. He would bring home small portions of Carbide in the hollow handle-bars of his bicycle. We accumulated several ounces of this interesting resource.

Vic would have fun in the Dock-yard toilet. Now let me explain. The toilets were a small row of cubicles each with a wooden seat. Situated under the seat was a small stream of water that would flow in a trough. Waste would be washed away very much in the style of old Roman times, clean and hygienic.

There was "No Smoking" in the Dockyard because of the munitions, so the men would sneak off for a smoke to the loo. The prankster would occupy the first toilet and when the others were in use he would sprinkle carbide into the can, when water and carbide are mixed the gas given of is highly inflammable. Just as he prepares to leave the loo, he drops a lighted match into the can. Many a bare back-side has been singed in this way and it is hard for a man with his pants around his ankles to catch a fleeing boy. Another time we made a bomb using a thick glass bottle with a screw cap. A hand-full of carbide in the bottle with a few ounces of water, screw on the lid, drop the bottle in a prepared hole then run for cover. When the thing exploded Mr. McAllister, our air raid warden, ran towards us shouting "Take Cover," as he ran along the hedge a rose briar dragged across his scalp. My, how he bled, we were scared we would be blamed. He didn't care though as later he received the George Cross for being injured in the course of duty.

I was a volunteer fire fighter. I applied to Mr. McAllister for a steel helmet, he told me "You can't have one until you are fourteen."

So instead I wore a woolen toque, it made me feel a bit safer, in hindsight, and I suppose ignorance is bliss. I would roam the streets, in our part of the city when the action was on-going and armed with a shovel I would cover burning incendiary bombs with earth to minimize damage. These bombs had an unpleasant way of throwing off showers of burning magnesium. Incendiary bombs were dropped in our residential area by the thousands in an indiscriminate way, I can tell you now, and they were a terrifying weapon.

Now, many years later when I hear the RAF being criticized for bombing Dresden and other German cities, I must say that memories of that time allow for little sympathy. It is strange to me how few seem to recall the suffering of the war-torn Brits. At night, lying in darkness in our cold shelters. We could hear the bombs whistling down and exploding. We could feel the ground shaking as the bombs got closer and closer. Then there would be a lull while we lay with our teeth clenched and waited for the next onslaught. Our Mother, holding Judy to her breast sitting by the exit singing Welsh lullabies, in an effort to soothe our fears.

The German planes made a different sort of noise than ours. Their engines seemed to be out of synchronization and this distinctive sound would warn us of trouble even prior to the air-raid sirens sounding the alarm. Night after night we would live through this terror and of course there were thousands and thousands who did not survive. One street down from Laurel Street, two Anderson shelters had been built with just a few feet between. A high explosive bomb had landed in the space between and all the eight children sleeping there had been killed. Their parents having tea in their house were spared. As I was helping to dig for the bodies of the kids, the whole horror of the situation struck me and I turned and ran from there. I found refuge and some peace in the Trelawney estate a few hundred yards from that dreadful abattoir.

Often staying home from school following a heavy raid, I would go around our area with my little go-cart collecting unexploded incendiary bombs, running messages or helping clean up. On one occasion I took an incendiary bomb home and using our back door as a vice, I removed a spring which I thought would de-fuse it. I threw it out my bedroom window and the thing exploded and destroyed my mother's new coco-fibre back door-mat. Eleven pence ha'penny gone up in smoke. I received a dose of the copper stick for that stupid action.

Early in the war we had a chance to meet personally some allied soldiers who had seen the Germans face to face. These were the days of Dunkirk. Down on the water-front we would help exhausted soldiers, some in tattered uniforms, and some still carrying their rifles. We would hold out our hands and help those tired men ashore. Sometimes we would be rewarded with a button torn from their uniform or a small French, coin. As I recall most of the men I saw were French. The weather, thank God was mild and most of those defeated men were able to get aboard a boat of some kind and make it to England's southern coast to safety.

Laurel Street produced several heroes. One was Mrs. Evans. Now there was a woman who commanded respect by her very presence. She is long gone now but in those hectic, brutal, yet wonderful days she would patrol her patch and with unusual energy, to protect all the local children from harm. She was short, stocky and determined. She seemed to me, a thirteen year old, to be an old lady but I imagine her to have been in her forties. When the siren would sound the alert with its fluctuating howl, she would make sure everyone was in their proper shelter. She'd arrange cups of tea, when tragedy struck she would dig for victims and succor the wounded and distraught. She was a working class woman, who when needed assumed an important, leadership role. The rich and powerful, our natural leaders were non-visible during those awful times.

In those days, the main form of communication was radio. We could not afford a radio but a company called "Redifussion" provided for a small, weekly, fee (I believe three-pence) a cable system which gave us two channels of entertainment/information. A switch on the front of the speaker allowed you to select A or B station. We would gather round the speaker in our living room and listen to the news, though often only static or muffled sounds were heard.

There were fourteen houses in our little Cul-De-Sac, ours was #8 Laurel Dene. The other half of our semi-detached house was occupied by Mr. and Mrs. Vowdan and their beautiful daughter Ivy. I would listen to Ivy practicing the piano and thought her to be wonderful, clever and ever so talented to create such lovely music. Mr. Vowdan used to buy horse manure from me. I charged two pence a bucket, eventually I developed the manure business into quite an income. I would deliver newspapers too, but I was fired from that job as I couldn't balance my accounts, however, I didn't mind losing that job as it paid only a few pence a week and was an awful lot of work.

Tom the baker hired me on Saturdays where we would deliver bread and other bakery supplies with a horse and cart. I'd earn sixpence for the half-day and Tom let me eat all the bread I wanted. Bread was 41/4 pence for a two pound loaf, in those days. The smell of fresh bread was wonderfully appetizing. Tom taught me that it was quite proper to pee down the back wheels of the wagon when having to relive oneself. We had a regular route of customers and sometimes to get from location to location we'd sit behind our huge beautiful horse as he gently trotted along. Tom would nudge me to watch the horse as the great animal quietly lifted its tail to expel flatus with a long hissing sound. I would count to see the length of time of the fart's duration. We would get the full benefit of the hot odor, but it was not as disgusting as you might think.

The neighbors' to our left were the Copps. There were nine of them. The dad was a navvy. Every evening he would come home dressed in his work clothes, his yellow corduroy trousers tied with string just below his knees. His hob-nailed boots striking noisily on the concrete footpath. I asked him once, "Why do you tie string around the knees of your pants?"

He informed me, "Well, you see I do it to prevent rats and mice from climbing up my trouser legs while I work in the ditches."

I thought I would never want to be in his shoes working at that job. We never heard any shouting from next door as he didn't raise his voice as his six, strong sons and seventeen year old daughter always seemed well behaved.

One of the boys, Albert, never spoke as he had been kicked in the head by a horse. The daughter had got into trouble, she was short and stocky and not very attractive. The boyfriend who now avoided her was confronted by the brothers plus the dad and pressure was brought to bear. The boy wasn't keen to marry as the girl was not pretty. The brothers gave the boy a nasty beating and later the two youngsters did get wed. (Meant one less little bastard was being born).

In those days there was an institution which was very popular "The Ford Bug House" this was a grubby, little, cinema which every Saturday presented movie matinee shows. Admittance was two pence for a seat in the stalls and three pence to be seated in the balcony. Kids could yell and cheer for their hero and scream their hearts out at the performance of heroes such as: Flash Gordon, Gene Autry, Tom Mix etc. It boiled down to two hours of fun and fantasy. Though sometimes a fight broke out when the kids in the balcony would throw water and sodas onto unsuspecting kids below.

The countryside around Plymouth was without a doubt the most beautiful in the world. We'd head over to the moors and camp out overnight. No one told you where to go or not go and people cleaned up after themselves and buried their litter.

There were a lot of wonderful places you could visit and Austin Fort was one of my favorites. Situated in a small valley behind the fort and I could pick arms full of bluebells to take home to my mother. Further on there were other places for adventure such as: Bere Ferrers, Mutley Plain and a whole new exciting world to explore. Further east of the city, there were other interesting places, across the moors you would reach Tavistock, Yelverton, Didworthy, St. Ives and Plympton. We would watch the ponies which ran wild in the area. And we walked along by the Roman Aqueduct which has been there for nearly two thousand years and if it's been protected from the developers it is probably still there.

During the peak of the air raids, thousands of people would leave our war-torn city for the night or week-end to escape the continual dangers. Sometimes Glyn and I would walk for miles out and continue walking up to Beacon Park Road and past Mutley Plain where the rich people lived. On one occasion we were given a lift in a military convoy, eventually we were put up in an officer's billet. Glyn and I were given a cup of hot Ovaltine by the officer's batman. Later, we watched the continual flashes of battle, light up the sky over the city of Plymouth, made soundless by the distance. Then fall into the arms of Morpheus and sleep the sleep of exhausted innocence. West of the city and across the River Tamer, the county of Cornwall also offered respite from the nightly torment of the war.

Plymouth Sound, near the bronze statue of Sir Francis Drake, lawn bowling still takes place. The Smeaton Lighthouse still stands and towards the Barbican the great Fort with its many cannons, still "protects" our beautiful city. Standing on the Hoe and looking out and eastward of the breakwater is Mountbatten, the home base of the Coastal Command Short, Sunderland, flying Boats. To see these giant craft taking off across the sound was a sight to behold. They would taxi for what seemed like miles before leaving the water and slowly fly out of sight, gleaming in the sun. These sights and the sounds of the thundering engines would thrill the dead.

A row of lovely terraced homes had been built in Victorian Times across the Hoe occupied by the wealthy elite. We were told that Lady Astor lived there. It was rumored that one of the houses left their windows without black-out curtains and the Luftwaffe could pinpoint their attacks with this aid, in their navigation. Lady Aster had been a minister of the Conservative government. Another Tory, Mr. Hore Belisha, was more fondly remembered for introducing roadway crosswalks known as Belisha Beacons.

Britain was under intense pressure at the time. Plymouth was probably the most bombed city in relation to its population. The downtown shopping district was very badly damaged, the beautiful department store called Spooner's was reduced to a pile of rubble and were conducting business in a Nisson Hut, not that there was much of anything for sale. There was one occasion following an air raid, school was closed. I went for a walk in the city ending up in the Spooner's Store, on one counter there was a pile of unwrapped merchandise that was on sale. I noticed a single glove on sale for sixpence. I remember staring at the glove, I didn't own a pair of gloves. I asked the lady clerk where is the other glove?

She replied "It had been lost."

I asked her "If she was looking for a one handed man to sell the glove to?" She called the manager and I was escorted out of the store.

Politicians and architects had produced a movie in which was described as the City of Plymouth that would be built after the war. I remember hearing adjectives like Utopian and Futuristic which were used to describe the new city. I haven't been back there since war time and I wonder if the new, improved city is good enough for those people who suffered so much to save it.

Central Park was the center-point for many activities. We would play or watch team sports. We'd fly our kites and model airplanes. One could play tennis, cricket or bowl, the children's area had swings, monkey bars, slides and seesaws. It was great. This huge park was maintained by our tax money and there was no entry fee or charges of any kind. At night it was awesome. The drone of the enemy aircraft, the searchlights, the bombs whistling down and the more staccato firing of the anti-aircraft gunfire. Once in a while a searchlight would catch and hold a plane and other lights and gunfire would converge on the plane until it was destroyed or disappeared into the clouds.

At night crossing the park during the action, with falling, spent shrapnel pattering onto the pavement including pieces, some pieces weighing several ounces. Sometimes we would collect pieces of this hardware if it had an interesting shape. I could have used a metal Helmet but as luck would have it I was never struck by this airborne flotsam. The city was ringed with Barrage Balloons. Sometimes we would see a German plane using them for target practice. Then they would burst into flames and come tumbling out of the sky like a massive firework. When there was no enemy aircraft around we would see our two Spitfires cruising around, I imagine this show was staged strictly for morale purposes.

One day while walking to school, right above our heads, a Dornier 17 (flying pencil) was engaged by a RAF plane and its tail was shot off. It seemed to carry on flying for a few seconds before it started to spin towards the ground, the two pilots bailed out and floated gently to earth. I watched 5 Junkers 88 flying over Central Park and saw a Gloucester Gladiator Plane shoot one out of the sky. Whenever these successes were observed by citizens they would cheer and toss their hats into the air. We loved the RAF boys and wanted to be like them when we were old enough

I would not have skipped the third year of high school, except for the fact that many of the younger teachers had joined the military and the balance of the students had been accelerated to accommodate staff shortages. I moved from 2B to 4B despite my lack of intellectual progress. Now as a fourth former I had teachers who took their job seriously and for whatever reason, the cane still occupied a prominent role in discipline. If a boy was not too bright, a dose of the cane was supposed to help! It must have been very stressful for a teacher to instruct up to forty, unruly, boys, many of whom would rather have been elsewhere.

I had been in the curriculum where the emphasis was on commerce rather than based on technology. Mr. Normington taught shorthand, typing and book-keeping. I remember the keyboard to this day but I could never get beyond the two-finger level for fear of the cane and that didn't seem to help. The boy at the bottom of the class sat in the back row. He was a big boy, at least a head taller than the teacher. On this occasion he had fallen asleep.

"Wake up boy," Normington yelled, then called him to the front and out into the corridor to wait for his six of the best. Normington followed the boy while flexing his cane. Many of the boys crowded around the windows overlooking the corridor to watch the punishment. We heard the swish and thwack of the cane, then repeated while Smithy blubbered. At the third stroke the crying boy grabbed the cane from the teachers grasp and began to hit him with it and it was frightening to see our elderly teacher running screaming to the principal's office to escape the maddened boy. Later the lesson was continued and Smith was expelled.

Mr. Clark was our vice principal and chief disciplinarian, and he also taught English and Music. He had a great deal of influence on our attitudes. The music we created was very inspiring. I remember even now the wonderful hymn "Tubal Cain" –

> And ye, oh sons of Tubal Cain,
> fire oh fire my soul and guide my hand.
> Lend me your aid, oh grace divine
> Fathers of old to whom we prayed
> Spirits of power be thy help mine
> Lend me you aid, lend me your aid.
> Etc...or words to that effect.

There were more than a hundred boys lustily singing in the auditorium. Mr. Clark, enrapt, standing on a chair leading us to greater efforts. He set us impossible tasks and we were exposed to inspiring and patriotic music and literature. Among our favorites was Tennyson's "Charge of The Light Brigade" and when reciting this magnificent poem who couldn't hear the roar of the cannons and the galloping hoof-beats, and smell the acrid stink of spent gunpowder. Every British man and boy could recite at least one verse...

> Half a league, half a league, Half a league onward
> All in the valley of death rode the six hundred
> "Forward the Light Brigade" was there a man dismayed
> Not though the soldier knew, someone had blundered.
> Theirs's is not to reason why, theirs is but to do or die
> Into the valley of death rode the six hundred

Stormed at with shot and shell, boldly they rode and well
Into the jaws of death, into the mouth of hell,
rode the six hundred.
And so on …

This poem and similar other pieces we would learn by heart and recite them in class, they would send shivers down my back. However, now it is time to move on. Our home is bombed beyond livability. Our nearest relatives are in Rhyl, North Wales. The authorities gave my mother a rail voucher to North Wales and ahead of us lay an exhausting journey of twenty hours. The train-ride to Rhyl was a blur. We slept and watched the country-side slide past. The train was packed with evacuees and military. How my mother coped I cannot imagine but it must have been hell for her.

We changed trains a number of times and eventually arrived at Aunt Elva's, the taxi from the station was a 1923 Rolls Royce. We arrived at Elva's, hungry, dirty and exhausted. We were fed and washed and found a place on the floor to sleep. The following day, the housing authorities expropriated two Gypsy Caravans for our use. Thus began a new and wonderful life for the entire family in this paradise, Golden Sands Holiday Camp, Kimnel Bay, Denbyshire, in beautiful North Wales.

War Memory, Plymouth, Devon

It doesn't take a lot of effort to take myself back to those terrible times. I can still hear the sirens and the throbbing engines of those waves of German bombers, the horrible scream of the falling bombs and the crump crump of our ack ack in a desperate effort to protect our city. I was twelve when the journey began, September, 1939 and that phase of the war lasted for me until my fourteenth birthday.

We all could write a book about those dreadful times. There were many unsung heroes, in fact I really believe that when pressed, the most unlikely can become a hero. I distinctly have memories of Mrs. Evans, a working class, short, chubby, middle-aged lady who appointed herself our local leader. She did magnificent work keeping us safe, or tried to.

She rounded up any children playing in the streets when the sirens sounded the alarm and made sure we were in our proper shelter. Later she was awarded the "George Cross" for her tireless efforts, fire-fighting, first-aid, cups of tea for the stressed and wounded. Then, there were many heroes.

Our government came up with two inventions to help protect the citizenry during the bombing, these were named after two government ministers, Morrison and Anderson Shelters. I will share my knowledge of these two devices in case you are unfamiliar with them.

The Morrison shelter was a small steel structure which had to be assembled in the house. About the size of a dining room table. When the action was on, those who were unable to move to a more safe location could crawl under the Morrison. They would take their bedding and their personal comforts and make the best of things when the bombing raids continued. The Anderson Shelter was quite different. We were one of the millions of families who were provided with an Anderson Shelter along with the instructions of how to erect the thing.

Our Anderson was dropped off at our front doorstep by a city truck. My father and I carted the pieces to our back yard near where we would dig a hole, about three feet deep in the clay. There we would bolt the parts together. It was terribly hard work digging that hole which was about ten by seven feet. There were eight pieces of curved, galvanized steel about seven feet high and thirty inches wide.

The first job was to dig the hole and level it three feet deep, then lay the foundation of four pieces of channeled steel, bolted together. Digging in that clay was very hard work, so my father would take off to the pub to replace his sweat, leaving me, a small, skinny twelve year-old kid to carry on. It took us a month to finish that hole. It was simple to assemble the shelter, the holes were all pre-drilled and ready and the pieces fitted together quite easily. The back was formed by three flat pieces of the same material. The front of the apparatus was a little different as there was a four foot by three foot entry, no door just an opening. When the package was assembled we double checked that all bolts were securely tightened.

The next step was to back-fill and cover the entire structure, with earth which we had excavated. About three feet in front of the access we built a wall of rocks and clay to deflect any possible bomb blast. We were instructed to cover the unit with three feet of earth but we were satisfied that a little less than two feet would be sufficient. The saved pieces of sod we used to cover the mound to prevent erosion.

Now to furnish the unit in preparation for our family use, we covered the earthen floor with duck-boards and laid old mattresses down, covered with sleeping bags and blankets. During heavy raids we would hunker down amongst the bedding and try to keep each other warm. I remember my mom would sit right by the exit and quietly sing old, Welsh lullabies to calm our fears.

My father was in the army and we seldom saw him. Sometimes when the bombs were close our shelter would shake and we were anxious that the shelter might collapse and we would all die. We would be stiff with the cold and shivering in our scant covers. Then in the morning we would make our way to school, on foot as often the buses would not be running. But it was only two miles away and sometimes we would see the enemy bombers heading home after their nasty work.

I could go on about that time in Plymouth. It was frightening yet at the same time it was exciting. Even though I was a young lad, I helped with fire-fighting, collecting unexploded incendiary bombs, cleaning up and generally helping where I was needed.

That phase of my war ended when that fateful heavy explosive device, a land mine, landed close by and destroyed our home, we felt the blast but we were all in our nearby shelter and we survived. We collected some of the pale green remnants of the parachute that had been attached to that awful bomb. The following day the entire family with the exception of my soldier father, were put on a train and evacuated to North Wales. Which is another, happier story.

Plymouth Navy Week 1938, (and an afterthought)

There are not a lot of people still alive, who can tell you about the show from their personal observation. I was there in 1938 and I still feel the thrill and amazement of my good fortune to have had that experience. I believe there may have been a "Navy Week" before that date but with certainty I tell you, there has never been one since. There is only one other exposition in the whole world where you can be thrilled to that extent, and that is the Kennedy Space Center, at Titusville, Florida. I have been there too and in many ways they both demonstrate man's tremendous achievements. The beauty of the American show is the fact that it is still there, available to be visited, for a modest cost. For a handful of dollars you can walk among the space travel hardware, and touch those vehicles which have been to other worlds.

Navy Week alas, is history. I was eleven years old. Most of us were poor and the idea of a shilling to pay the entrance fee was unimaginable, but there are more ways to skin a cat, as the saying goes. Young boys are by nature very adventurous and not having a shilling did not deter our expectations, my pals and I were going to see everything that was on display.

The British Navy ruled the waves, and it behooved the champions to show to the world the Royal Navy in all its splendor. Plymouth and the Devonport docks was the venue. The entire area was contained by a wall and on the wall there was an iron fence that was six feet in height. I remember those big iron rails shaped like stubby lances and painted black, the pointed tops tipped with gold. They were designed to be too close together to squeeze through, but by helping each other we were able to climb over the fence and into the exhibition. For one glorious week the great iron gates were opened and the public allowed entry. The first ships to be seen, introducing us to the fleet, were the aircraft carriers, and the first of those was the magnificent HMS Ark Royal.

Then in the nearby dock was the HMS Eagle the sister ship of the ARK Royal. Later, we walked the deck of a third Carrier, the HMS Argus, there lined up on their decks were the airplanes which flew from them. Front and center on their flight deck was the Fairy Swordfish, with its torpedo mounted between it's under carriage. We walked on the huge flight deck and experienced a ride on the elevator, which was about the size of a tennis court. Two planes and several sailors were on that deck and the sailors seemed to be busy keeping the crowd of tourists safe. The lift slowly lowered from the flight deck to the work deck below, nearly twenty feet down, which took the planes from the flight deck to the hangar beneath.

All around were uniformed, friendly, sailors, anxious to describe their ship and her weapons to anyone who expressed an interest. Thousands of visitors carrying their cameras walked the decks of those ships and I wondered how many were spies recording secret information. There were great battleships, The HMS Hood and the HMS Rodney and others, with their huge, 16 inch guns looking so alert and at the ready. There was even a cruiser which carried ahead of her bridge, a Fairy Swordfish plane, mounted in a form of catapult.

"How would the plane get back on the ship when it had finished its work and where would it land?" I asked the Petty Officer in charge.

"Well son" the Officer replied, "The Pilot would locate a place on land or land in the sea, beside the ship. Those big floats you see there on the plane, allow it to land on water, then it would be winched aboard." I stayed for a while and watched while a crew came to service that beautiful, little plane, but nothing exciting was happening so I continued on my adventure.

We not only walked the decks and gun turrets but below decks we examined the crew's quarters and the shining engine-room. It smelled strongly of oil, and of course we viewed the galley, from where more than a thousand ships-company were fed. One of the sailors gave me a piece of fresh bread to eat, starving like a wolf I quickly swallowed it and took a second piece and placed it in my pocket for Gerald for when

I ran into him again. How neat and clean everything was, and I noticed how friendly and sharing the crew seemed to be. They shared their cigarettes and tobacco with me and at eleven I smoked my first cigarette. I can still remember how nauseated it made me feel. In the galley I was given samples of ships cocoa, which was cocoa and sugar pressed into blocks. Cocoa was a common beverage served to sailors when on watch duty, in cold weather. The block of cocoa would be melted in boiling water and the sweet frothy mixture would be served in large mugs. From time to time, for the rest of the day when hunger pangs hit me I would take that lump of ships-cocoa from my pocket and suck it for a while to stave off my hunger. I still remember its bitter-sweet flavor and its gritty texture.

We visitors were allowed to wander around the ships, there were no restrictions. I found my way into a 16 inch gun turret where an exercise was in progress. Great packs of gunpowder and a shell weighing a ton, were brought by a lift apparatus, from deep in the bowels of the ship. We listened enrapt while the gunnery-officer's orders were carried out by the team of sailors.

Every member of the gun crew was wearing a type of helmet covering his head and ears. This was normal attire as the thunderous noise of the firing guns would deafen a man at the first volley. On this day, of course, only the routines were being followed. It was explained to us that the armory housing the shells was located in the remotest part of the ship, for safety purposes, during battle. There in a nearby drydock was an old ship being re-fitted, the HMS Colombo. It looked out of place amidst the giant fighting ships. We were not allowed on the Colombo, however, it didn't look very interesting anyway.

Further along in a great wet-dock, triple-moored, were three H class destroyers, the HMS Fame, Fearless and Foresight. The outermost ship, the Foresight, was crowded with sightseers, as a display of torpedo firing was to take place. Now for some exciting action. The HMS Seahorse, a small submarine, was to be the enemy today as the Foresight would fire one of her torpedoes directly at her. This simulated battle was being watched by thousands, and I of course being small and inquisitive was able to find a place close to the action. The torpedo firing device was like a large rack, in which four torpedoes were housed. A sailor sat on top of the frame and by turning a handle he could point the unit in the desired direction. The instructions to the crew were coming over the public address system in a loud, clear, voice, then when the torpedo was aimed the voice spoke loudly.

"I see, near the torpedo a small boy wearing a pink shirt, sandals and torn khaki shorts, perhaps he would like to fire the torpedo?"

I looked around me for a few seconds then I screamed out "It's me, it's me."

I ran to the firing station and took a seat beside the sailor in charge of the firing. Then came the order over the Tannoy, "Fire" it called. I pulled the lanyard firing trigger and with a mighty "whoosh," a charge of compressed air shot the projectile into the basin toward the submarine.

I felt like a hero listening to all those cheering voices as I made my way to other ships needing my attention. I wish I had a photo of myself taken that day. I was eleven plus a few months old and I was small, skinny, dirty and sunbaked, and oh so happy and free. Most of the time there, I spent with my best pal, Gerald Teague. Gerald was a year older than me and had more life's experiences. I fell off a work-raft into one of the docks and it was Gerald who saved me from drowning, but boys aren't Siamese twins and we did become separated. I ended up attending a free movie in the dockyard, one of the amenities usually reserved for naval officers and men. Today a wonderful movie was playing, "Life on the Ocean Waves" with Tommy Trinder. I smoked some of the cigarettes that were given me as I watched that movie, then became quite ill and barely made it to the toilet.

There was an area where figure-heads of old sailing "ships of the line" were mounted and each had a plaque describing that ship's history. Of course, a friendly sailor was ready and willing to bring that story to life. Some of those carved figure-heads were more than twice as big as a man, and beautifully painted and decorated with gold leaf. I remember one carving of Britannia, and I imagined her on the prow of a great "ship of the line" square-rigged and under sail, sweeping our enemies from the sea. What a thrill to see such power and to be part of it.

What a wonderful day in the summer sunshine, not one thought of the dark clouds of war gathering on the horizon. Not a thought of the rumbling of activity in the shipyards of Germany as Hitler was preparing for war. He planned to wipe the British Navy from the sea, using Germany's secret weapons being mass-produced, the pocket-battleships and the worst killers of all, the U-Boats. In thinking back to that time, in history there was no anger or shouting, no complaints or criticism. There was no fighting or drunkenness, no police display of authority, no mace or Tasers and yet there were thousands upon thousands of people milling about. In a way, it was similar to the Space display in Florida.

Yes, one year, and a month later, Britain was at war, and what a dreadful toll was taken on British shipping and so many thousands died. The pocket-battleships did their terrible work, and the U-Boats, the scourge of the seas, hunted the allied convoys, sinking hundreds of thousands of tons of ships that were bringing food and supplies to the war-torn Brits.

Eventually, the secret German cipher machine "Enigma" was neutralized by the British Boffins and in 1943 the Wolf-Packs of U-Boats were withdrawn from the North Atlantic. The famous HMS Hood foundered beneath the grey Atlantic and only three men survived while over a thousand sailors perished. This was probably the lowest point of pride and morale of the British people. Some prestige returned when the pocket battle-ships, the Bismark and the Tirpitz were destroyed.

My friend Gerald Teague, joined the Royal Navy, early in the war, he was just fourteen. How that came about was not an unusual story. Gerald's dad was a sailor on the armed merchantman HMS Rawlpindi. Sadly, that ship was sunk by the Pocket Battleship Deutschland early in the war. She was shelled and sunk by the Deutschland with all hands and passengers lost.

The range of the German ship's great guns was able to reach out to the unsuspecting Rawalpindi while still several miles out of range of the smaller ship's armament. As a result of this action, the Royal Navy offered to take Gerald under its care as a boy-seaman. A few years ago I wrote to the Admiralty in Whitehall and attempted to get in touch with my boyhood friend. I received a reply indicating that Gerald had left the Navy in 1955, and they had no knowledge of his whereabouts. Even though I regretted the news I was gratified to hear that he had survived the dreadful war.

Later, in the late fall of 1939, I was fishing on the pier at the Barbican, in Plymouth. I seemed to be taking forever to grow and be able to join the ranks of the Royal Navy. There, slowly sailing past me was the HMS Exeter, limping into her home port after her business with the Graf Spee off the port of Montevideo. Sailors dressed in their number one whites lined the deck of the brave little fighting ship and her ship's band played joyous music.

A crowd of several thousand had collected on the shoreline and cheered as the ship sailed past, hardly making way. How gallantly she, along with the Ajax and Achilles, had fought, engaging the Pocket Battleship (Panzershiff), The Admiral Graf Spee. The Exeter was almost destroyed during that terrible battle and her crew was decimated, but there she was, all patched up with canvas and plywood, to hide the dreadful damage to her armor and superstructure. She was moving along, under her own steam to Devonport to be re-fitted. Eventually, the captain of the Graf Spee, in order not to suffer the disgrace of defeat at the hands of those smaller, Royal, Naval, ships, ordered his crew to abandon ship as his scuttled, monstrous, ship sank in the cold, grey, South Atlantic Ocean.

Thank God for the Commonwealth, friends, and the United States of America, and the heroic efforts of a proud and loyal people. We finally prevailed in that horrible conflict, and the Third Reich, which was to last a thousand years, was defeated.

A sad post script to this dreadful affair was that the commander of the Graf Spee, later, was to take his own life.

Church Outing
Looe, Cornwall – 1938

Once each year, the Methodist Church, to which I belonged, had a bus outing to the sea-side for all the children of the congregation. Father Cockeral, our minister, was a great, big, kindly man, always dressed in his uniform which consisted of his four-cornered, tasseled hat, white dog-collar and his long black suit with the skirt almost touching the ground.

I was in the choir of his little wooden Church. I added to the size of the choir however, my musical talent was restricted to working the big lever which provided air to the old-fashioned, Church organ. The organist was a mean, old, lady, stooped and sharp-featured. She constantly scolded me and hissed out of the corner of her mouth, for me to pump faster. She would also hiss at me to stop talking to my sister while Father Cockeral was giving his sermon. It didn't take me long to realize that I could make her go through the hissing routine whenever I wanted. I tested this theory and made her very angry and frustrated. I certainly caused her a lot of annoyance.

As I recall, I was eleven when this outing took place. As an undersized, ragged boy, usually found with a snotty nose and in need of a haircut, at the same time I was eager and would respond to kindness, without thought or hesitation. This year the Church outing was to be Looe, Cornwall. Looe was an unusually charming fishing village built around a fiord-like crack in the coastline. It was located about twenty miles west of Plymouth. On the side of the steep inlet, about a quarter of a mile inland, picturesque cottages were perched. There were cliffs, lovely flowers and trees, several shops and of course the inevitable Churches and public-houses.

There was the Methodist Church near the center of the village. Best of all, attached to the Church was a large hall which was set up to feed and entertain two bus-loads of noisy, vociferous, children. I believe there must have been nearly eighty of us on that trip, including several mothers enlisted as our chaperones to watch over us and keep us in line.

All the children were happy to escape for the day. We met at the Church in Swilly and the buses were loaded. Our journey took about two hours including the ferry ride, across the River Tamer at Saltash. We arrived in relatively, good condition due to the vigilance of our guards. We were famished and thirsty, having exhausted ourselves singing hymns, for most of the ride. We were told to explore the village and be back at four o'clock for tea. My nemesis had told me to take care as she was keeping an eye on me for my mother. Anyway, the crowd of happy kids dispersed, and was divided into hunting parties and we headed out for a fun adventure.

Naturally, every kid had his own vision of the day. My day was highly exciting. I walked every inch of the village and explored every shop, even though I had no spending money. I walked down to the water's edge where the fishing boats were laying on their sides, in the estuary's mud. It was low tide. I met several old fishermen, most of whom were big, fat and bearded. They were very friendly, elderly, men who were glad to have an audience. Though I was just a lad from the city who could be regaled with their fishing stories.

One old chap whose name was Captain, told me that several years ago, a huge shark had entered their port and for several days had cruised to and fro and succeeded in upsetting village life. Eventually, he and a friend were commissioned to kill it, or get rid of the giant shark, somehow. They accomplished this task by gathering a few friends, with loaded guns to join them on their fishing boat. They cruised up and down the river, while shooting at the target whenever they caught sight of it. The great fish eventually got tired of being peppered with gunshot and departed for more peaceful waters, never to be seen again.

Then another old man told me a story about a giant, killer octopus. This "tall" tale even I found hard to believe.

It was one of those days that it was great to be a kid. The sun shone from a clear blue sky, it was warm but an on-shore breeze kept us feeling comfortable. The village was like a picturesque postcard, so clean and neat. I climbed to the top of the cliff, overlooking the village and watched the people below. They seemed so small, in the distance merely going about their business. It was great to be alive in England. Suddenly, away in the distance the Anglican Church tower struck four o'clock. Like Cinderella leaving the ball at midnight, I fled my overlook and made all haste for tea time. It didn't take me long, as Looe is not a big place.

The last of the children were entering the big hall, I was seated with the other eleven-year-olds, on a long bench, at the end of a huge table. We were given a large bottle of lemonade with a straw and a good-sized ham roll. The bread was thick and chewy and swimming with butter and thin slices of ham - it was so delicious.

Stacked at the end of the table were the desserts. You could smell the strawberry preserves on those fresh, sweet rolls, topped with a big blob of whipped cream. You would have to be dead for your mouth not to water in anticipation. We were all given our jam rolls and there was utter silence except for the moans of enjoyment. We cleaned up carefully licking our fingers and the paper plates to make sure we had devoured the last morsel. To finish up the wonderful feast we were each given a mug of warm, sweet, tea.

On the tray just beside me, there was one surplus strawberry bun. I had been eyeing it with longing. Someone had to have it.

A caretaker asked me if I would like to have a second bun.

I replied "Yes, please Miss," then another mother took the bun and gave it to the nicely dressed, fat, curly-haired boy, sitting across from me. Disappointment must have been written all over my face.

Next year, that's when the war broke out, we all went to Yelverton, Devon. That's where I saw a river full of milk. Next time I will tell you all about that adventure.

Doctor Jones Senior - 1941

Like most boys of fourteen I was innocent and naïve. We lived in North Wales in a place called "Golden Sand." Most of my clothes were hand-me-downs as a result of wartime shortages on the one hand and poverty on the other. I had one pair of trousers and I tried my best to keep them in good repair, however, like most active, teenaged, boys at that time I found this to be quite difficult. Though I was young and innocent, in many ways I was clever and able. I could hunt and provide meat for our family; I could fish and sell my catch from door to door and give my mother some badly needed cash. I could be taken advantage of but most of the time boys like me were treated fairly and with kindness.

I enjoyed amazingly good health despite what had been an inadequate diet and at this crucial stage of my life I was growing at an alarming rate. I remember this as being one of the happiest and most exciting adventures of my life. Not a day went by without some new experience, or reading some interesting book which broadened my knowledge of the world and its people. I had recently left school but it seemed to me that now my real education had just begun.

Though I was rarely ill, once in a while I had to visit our family doctor whose office was in his beautiful home, in Kimnel Bay. Doctor Jones, senior, and his son Doctor Jones junior had a busy practice in that part of town.

They were widely known for their kindness and thoughtful care. Dr. Jones sr., was a very short, round, bald, elderly, man. His son Dr. Jones jr., was quite the opposite, being a man of around forty, tall, and thin with an enormous head of dark hair. There the differences ended; they both had been missionary evangelistic Doctors and had spent many years in China. Just before the outbreak of World War Two they had left their Chinese, Christian, flock and returned to Wales and established this much needed medical practice.

I had been very impressed by the souvenirs decorating the lovely home and surgery. I was awed by the religious icons and symbols, especially as my leanings were more of an atheistic bent. I really couldn't understand how grown-up, educated, people could believe such obvious tales, but to each his own.

Trousers in those days, in Britain, did not have zippers like we have today. The trousers' fly was closed by three or four buttons. I had lost first one button from my fly, then another, then as a third came adrift, to maintain my modesty, I used safety pins in place of the lost buttons. On one occasion, struggling with a pin after using the bathroom, I did myself an injury to my private part.

The pain for the next day or two was fairly unpleasant and I decided to see Doctor Jones. I had heard about horrible diseases caused by sexual interaction and I diagnosed myself as having an early stage of syphilis.

I looked up the term in an old medical book and was horrified to learn the seriousness of my disease. I thought I must see my doctor. I went to Dr. Jones's office and was about to knock on his surgery door when I stopped short; how could I ask this very genteel, religious man about such disgusting things? I hurried away and walked up and down the beach in an agony of torment. Finally, I plucked up enough courage and realizing the life or death crisis I was in, then I returned and knocked on Dr. Jones's Surgery door.

Mrs. Jones Senior opened the door and I stepped inside. I sat in the almost empty waiting room and when my turn came Doctor Jones sr. invited me into his examining room.

"You're Mrs. Trower's boy Trevor, aren't you?" he said with a kindly smile.

"Yes Doctor Jones," I replied.

"Well, how are you Trevor?" continued Dr. Jones.

"Fine, thank you," I replied, wondering how I could tell him about my problem. Dr. Jones

Looked at his watch and said. "Come on Trevor, what's wrong?"

"It's my penis, Dr. Jones, I think I've got syphilis," I blurted out.

"Well, well, well, hmmmm" he said; "I better have a look."

In shame I undid the safety pin on my fly and lowered my pants.

"Have you ever been with a woman?" "No" I replied, "I'm only four-teen," I added; "I thought, what a question to ask."

The doctor finished his brief examination, "You haven't got syphilis or anything else; keep it clean and it will heal in a day or two."

A tremendous feeling of relief washed over me; Mrs. Jones Sr. showed me to the door and did not ask me to pay the two shilling fee. As I was leaving Dr. Jones came to the door and with one last piece of advice called out, "Oh Trevor, when you get home ask your mother to sew a couple of buttons on your trousers."

Me And Space

I remember as a small boy, I had an enormous amount of freedom. Maybe the fact that being one of a family of eight children had something to do with it.

Actually, there was only my mother to watch over us. It was impossible to give each of us any more attention than we received. Not that we ran wild exactly, but in my case I could investigate nature and think about life and the universe.

I can recall as if yesterday, the war raging in Plymouth, England, and the nightmares I could tell no-one about. Every-one seemed to have more and worse troubles than me. Rather I might say, they saw their problems with more self-concern than I did. I must have been thirteen years of age when I had my first experience of space.

Laying back among the thick comfortable grass in Central Park, I spent a long time staring at the late night sky. I remember trying to count the 'shooting stars' but there were so many that night that I soon lost count. As I stared at the sky, more and more stars seemed to fill the void. Until as my eyes became accustomed to the purple night, nearly all of the sky seemed filled with myriads of lights.

It appeared to me that many of those stars were close together, almost touching, yet in reality were light-years apart, in a third dimension. I, alone was a spark of life, watching the sky as it was, millions, no, billions of years ago.

I felt in the scheme of things the most powerful of we mortals, is as important as a speck of dust in comparison to the grandeur of the universe. My own troubles, and the difficulties of our family, began to fade into the distance.

Flash Gordon in the form of actor Buster Crabbe, was one of my boy-hood heroes and mostly his movies dealt with fantastic trips through space. It didn't take much imagination to travel with him on his Rocket-Ship to Mars. To fight the evil Martian, Lord Mung. Do you remember how we battled those awful Clay-Men and rescued the beautiful Princess held prisoner in those fearful dungeons? You can travel through space, in your thoughts, living an incredible life amongst the stars, and still be home for supper.

Even today it makes me smile to see examples of arrogance. How ridiculous to assume such self-importance being displayed by some society leaders. When the rich and powerful and social climbers look down their noses at those less fortunate, yet it's so much worse for those in need, to hero-worship those with power. To stand for hours in any kind of weather, for the questionable thrill of a glimpse of that famous personage. I still don't understand this mind set.

Years ago, a workmate friend, old Herbert Rothwell, told me that the lowliest and most Royal, all look the same with their clothes off. Suppose you are feeling any sense of awe, imagine them in their birthday suits, sitting on the toilet, straining for relief. No-one should be enslaved by tradition. Those who enjoy privilege by Divine Right, do so as a result of a huge con job. I believe it's a scam of such enormous proportion that it can almost be admired.

Unfortunately, for most people the freedom to travel in space is simply not an option. Though a few have spent their millions for that awesome ride and carry the honor of being an astronaut. Situated in the science museum in London, on the second floor, near the cockpit of the Vanguard, is one of the infamous V2 rockets.

This model wreaked such havoc during the final days of World War II. You can actually touch that display which is the forerunner of a spatial flight. Werner Von Braun, one of our most bitter enemies, was transferred to the USA and became a leading player in America's space race. Soon, many modern day heroes are men and women living real-life as astronauts, not in a motion picture, or computer-generated fantasy.

Take a trip as millions have, to the Kennedy Space Center in Florida. Walk around that space-park, completely free, without hindrance and live your own personal fantasy of travel through space. At the nearby IMAX Theater, you can watch an enormous screen showing the "Voyage of Discovery." The sights and sounds of leaving earth will hold you entranced and twisting in your seat, as the huge space-ship turns and thunders into space.

My trip all those years ago, though enjoyable, was only fantasy. To me the future holds a thousand more surprises. Whatever man's brain can conceive, however impossible, it is only a matter of time before man's hands can make it become a reality.

When I was a boy we would make our walkie-talkie phones out of string and tin cans, of course they didn't work. We had to shout so as our friend on the other end of the line could hear. Today, children walk to school or to the mall, chatting away on their cell phones which sends voice messages over cyberspace, to anywhere in the world. Astoundingly transmits and receives pictures in living color of the participants. Dick Tracy, in the thirty's, had amongst his fantastic gear a telephone/ television wrist-watch. Today these magical devices are available for everyone at a reasonable cost. Every new invention seems to lead to several more. Yet it seems to me these products were first introduced in a previous century in the stories of H. G. Wells, Ryder Haggard and Jules Verne.

I believe I was about fifteen when I entered the underground, mysterious world of Edgar Rice-Boroughs's and discovered "She," and came face to face with the author's Queen. I remember walking down those long, huge caves lit by great torches that never burned out. There was a fountain and lovely waterfalls surrounded by crowds of dancing, cheering, citizens.

When suddenly on a dais, like a Greek Goddess, was the beautiful Ayesha, (She who must be obeyed), like an alabaster living statue. She was dressed in diaphanous flowing silken robes. I remember the scenario quite well. She lowered her slender arms out toward me and a hush came over the gathered throng.

I stopped at her feet and stared at her violet eyes in awe as she glided down to where I was transfixed, with her incredible beauty. I lifted my arms to take those soft white hands in mine. I knew I would die in an instant if she wanted me. The vast crowd became silent as a smile lit up her exquisite face. Suddenly the entire cavern blackened and she disappeared. I was instantly smitten by a terrible sadness and loss, as I rushed about the darkness searching to find that heavenly creature.

Then I realized that she really didn't exist, she was a product of my imagination. It seemed for a long time that I rushed about frightened and frustrated.

Suddenly, something seemed to strike me in the chest, clothes seemed to be smothering me as I fought to escape, the pain in my chest became stronger and more insistent. I forced my eyes open while I heard the voice of my younger brother Glyn, calling, "Trev, Trev, for God's sake, you're taking all the bed-clothes and I'm freezing."

Sunday School
Outing to Yelverton

We kids always looked forward to our Church outings. As it was a reward of sorts for suffering through Sunday school, all year long. We didn't realize it at the time, but war would be declared in less than a month. As usual, we would meet at St Hilda's Methodist Church, in Swilly, a few blocks from our home, and board the buses for our big outing.

Yelverton, Devon, was a small, beautiful town on the moors, maybe twenty miles or so from our house in the city. I had explored the moors before, way up past Beacon Park Road and Mutley Plain, past the big houses where the rich people resided. I thrived on the thrill of the great, open spaces and the freedom of adventure. Catching rabbits, stealing potatoes and baking them in the ground till they were burnt black, then cracking open the burnt spud to find the fluffy, white, insides spilling out. Of course, with a large family on our meager budget I never had baked potatoes at home. How sad it is that children of today can't experience the lonely thrill of expedition. They can't escape the scrutiny of their parents concerned that some predator would do them harm.

The bus-ride that day was under way. Two loads of happy kids with several mothers as chaperones, to watch over us and tend to our wounds. As usual we sang cheerful hymns, adding our own naughty words whenever our creative juices could find an alternate for those words of reverence. A sharp, smack on the head was received for any kid found guilty. Yet those bus-rides were part of the fun and a smack on the head was a small price to pay. It's only today, many years later, that I wonder how the driver coped. Perhaps in those days people were made of hardier stock.

Our first stop was "The Rock," a few miles within the boundary of the Moors. This was an enormous, solitary stone located near the roadway, in the middle of nowhere. An obvious anomaly sitting as it was on that huge expanse of undulating land. Twenty feet high by thirty by forty. We were let off the bus and rushed to the nearby toilets, for relief. We went around the rock admiring its unusual form and looking for ways to get to its top.

"We don't want anyone climbing the rock or you'll get no tea," shouted several of our tenders. Oh, too late, my friend was half way to the top when I heard the warning, but if it is a choice between tea or the rock there is no contest. Up the rock I scrambled after my friend, followed by several other of the more adventurous boys. We lined the top of the rock and hurled jeers and scorn at those below. The caretakers were very upset at our wickedness. Finally, we were rounded up and amid the threats we continued on our bus ride.

Dartmoor is a National Park. Having within its confines hundreds of square miles of territory, including: some farming, villages and small towns. It is fenced however, there are no gates. This is the home of the Dartmoor Pony. The ponies flourish in this lovely place and tend to stay within the moors, as if it is their natural habitat.

There is an odd type of gate, those metal grills laid into the roadbed, which animals will not cross. As we drove across the moors with our noses pressed against the windows, we could see groups of ponies wandering about. There were hundreds of them. Some of us declared that we would come back later to catch one, and take it home. We learned that the public could apply to the park authorities for a license, to catch a pony and it was this method that the animals' number was kept under control.

Tavistock is the major town in this area and we heard that this was to be one of our stops. It is a beautiful market town with many lovely historic buildings. We didn't stay long as another treat was in store for us. Back into the bus and a half hour later we pulled up and parked beside a river, way up in the hilly part of the moor. River Plym, which ultimately finds its way to Plymouth.

We were down at the river's edge fascinated by the flowing stream which was quite white in colour. Our leaders told us that the source of the water was the chalk hills nearby and this same chalk was used to make the fine porcelain which the country is famous for.

We stayed for a while enjoying the scenery on our way to Yelverton and for some tea. The Methodist Church in Yelverton was willing to look after nearly eighty boys and girls between the ages of ten and thirteen. All of us of course arrived with enormous appetites. The church basement was prepared for a giant feast. A great urn of weak tea with sugar and Nestle's milk, and enough sandwiches of thinly-sliced ham, and butter, nestled between thick slices of fresh, white, country bread. There was enough food to feed a small army.

We had had a long day and we did honest work to that great mound of food. But you know, no matter how stuffed a kid might be, there is always a crevasse to be found for something sweet. Enormous fruit cakes were brought in for our dessert, full of raisins, cherries and candied peel. We ate and drank our cups of sweet tea while our host priest walked up and down our ranks, smiling and encouraging us to enjoy ourselves.

What a marvelous day. We were allowed to roam around the small town exploring, and were told that the buses would depart at six. Groups of children had formed, by those who had similar interests and together we strolled the cobbled roads of that historic place.

We found our way to the cliff-top overlooking the English Channel and watched the ships way off in the distance. The closer they were to the shore, the faster they seemed to travel. One could lay on the grass, on your back and watch the larks spiraling upward into space, singing away, without a care in the world. Our world was at peace.

We didn't have a watch, yet somehow our senses told us it was time to go and we gathered around our buses telling each other how much fun we had. We drove home by a different route, for a change of scenery, down by the coast and through several towns and villages. Eventually, we arrived at St Hilda's, our Church in Swilly. Some parents were waiting to take their children home, but most, like me, made their way home alone. More food was waiting for me at home and I ate again while I told my Mom about my marvelous day.

Spitfire – 1942

Just west of Rhyl where the River Clwyd enters the sea, the beach for several miles had been secured against its use by the Germans, as an aircraft landing field. What had been constructed was a rather unusual but simple protection system. Between low and high tide the golden, sandy, beach had been randomly spiked with hundreds of sturdy, wooden, poles. They were approximately fifteen to eighteen feet in length and separated about fifty yards apart.

This beautiful coast, at low tide exposed around a half mile of firm, sandy, beach which was several miles in length. Unfortunately, it was vulnerable to any airborne attack. The beach was protected early after the outbreak of hostilities in late 1939. Posts were dug and sunk into the sand several feet deep. Though the sea conditions, most of the time were unpleasantly rough, the posts withstood the wave action to a very high degree.

At low tide I'd often secure my baited, fishing lines between two of these posts and when the tide had flowed and ebbed, in a short time, I would then collect my catch of the day, which included various types of fish. Then I would sell them to my neighbors.

I vividly recall this day; the event was a clear, moving, picture, indelibly printed in my mind. A modest breeze was on-shore and the grey, seas, waves were perhaps two and a half feet high. The tide was rapidly receding and by now was nearly three quarters toward its lowest point.

Royal Air Force pilots often would fly their training missions, low-level practice, flying over the beaches, in our vicinity. As a fifteen-year-old, I'd watch in awe as I prepared my fishing lines on the beach, as the aircraft roared by, only a few yards above the sand.

I'd try to catch the pilot's eye by waving frantically for recognition.

What a treat it was, to have the young hero return my wave. My personal wish, for my own future was that the war would last long enough for me to enlist and become a fighter pilot.

I remember this event, though not the exact date. It was a Spitfire, on a low-level, training mission, hurtling above the River Clwyd, toward the open sea. As the plane passed over the Vorryd Bridge, its altitude dropped to just a few feet above the water. I watched this maneuver from about three hundred yards away.

Suddenly the aircraft seemed to touch a wave top, give a small bounce and splash into the water upside down, a spray of water and steam obscuring the accident scene. It was over in a few seconds. One moment the fighter's powerful, Rolls Royce engine, was thrilling the passers-by, and the next, shocked silence.

The aircraft upside down, the tail and rear part of the airframe visible above the waves. No sign of life and the golden beach stretching a half mile from the sea-wall to the waters edge. I stood transfixed, awed by the scene. A small crowd had gathered on the sea-wall promenade.

As I watched the scene unfold, still stunned, separating itself from the throng of folks viewing the happenings from the sea-wall, a lone figure of a man was clearly visible, charging toward the wrecked craft. Every few seconds the running man would divest himself of an article of clothing, jacket, tie, shirt would be cast off, while the others looked on. The man ran fast, his arms pumping and his head held back. He flew across the sandy beach, a single runner.

Without lessening speed or making any hesitation, he hurled himself into the water with a splash and began to swim, overarm style, out into the bitter, cold, water, to the still visible plane. The tide had almost reached its nadir when the man swam beside the plane, he paused for a moment, then dived underwater.

After a few seconds you could see the man's head re-appear; at the same time a small crowd had come down from the sea-wall, onto the beach and were slowly making their way across the sand. Soon they began to converge to a point at the water's edge, closest to the downed plane.

I was by now fairly close to the scene, but kept my distance away due to the deep water of the River Clwyd, as it intersected the beach and flowed into the sea.

The lone swimmer dived again, under the plane and seemed to re-main underwater for a long time. Suddenly, he re-appeared and now you could clearly see that the swimmer had retrieved the flyer from the wreck. He was starting to tow the unconscious pilot toward the safety of the shore. Now only fifty yards from shore, the crowd of maybe a hundred or more began to wade into the shallows, to help.

Only a minute or so more and the rescuer and pilot were engulfed by the crowd, gathered at the waters edge. The pilot was revived and still wearing his soaked, sheepskin, jacket. He was carried shoulder high by the happy throng. I noticed that the flyer was quite active now, responding to the crowd, with smiles and waves. An ambulance was waiting, on the road and took the pilot to the Royal Alexandra Hospital, away from the cheering crowd, who then began to disperse.

Meanwhile, back at the water's edge the hero of the lifesaving event was slowly recovering from his tremendous ordeal. He had exhausted himself in saving the pilot who had been stunned, but not badly hurt.

During the rescuer's second dive, miraculously he had located the cockpit, had unfastened the pilot's safety harness. Then, proceeded to pull him out of the cockpit and in doing so had saved his life. Two or three people had stayed to help the lifesaver as he slowly returned to normality, they supported and lifted him across the sand and assisted him in gathering up his pieces of clothing.

This was the second crash I had observed in this area, the previous one happened about six months earlier. It was a Bolton Paul Defiant plane; it was destroyed in almost identical circumstances, sadly that pilot had not survived.

I was a fifteen year old boy, fascinated with the wreck of the aircraft. Soon the police and military would become involved with the downed plane. Anything I could do I must do at once. By now the Spitfire was in water as shallow as it would become. About one half of the plane's frame was above water.

Into the water I went and waded and swam out to investigate. I found that the port wing had been quite badly ruptured and spilling out of its gun stowage was a long, brassy, belt of 303 ammunition; it had ejected itself from the wing and was there, waiting for me. I picked up the belt of shells and draped it around my neck, then proceeded to head for home.

I remember being quite upset when accosted by the police and I received awful threats of cruel punishment and was relieved of my prize, however, a few loose shells that I had sequestered in my pocket remained hidden.

That was the last I heard from the authorities in regard to the whole matter, though I lived in a state of funk, for a few days. I tried to fire my cartridges by inserting a bullet in a suitable post-hole, and with a nail and hammer attempted to use the nail as a firing pin without success (thank goodness). In disgust, I gave my remaining bullets to the guard on duty at the Kimnel Bay army camp.

St. Asaph, North Wales - 1943

I often associate places with events. In the case of St. Asaph, there is one particular event that never fails to make me realize that my boyhood was somewhat...different.

However, first, a description: St. Asaph is the smallest city in Wales. The River Clwyd, which enters the sea at the coastal town of Rhyl about fifteen miles to its north, is fresh water and, like with most communities, was the reason this place came into its existence. A few miles closer to the sea, the river is tidal, and saltwater fish often find their way there. This is a beautiful stretch of country, and the river meanders slowly to the north through rich farmland and meadows where herds of cattle provide a living. Huge trees on the riverside in St. Asaph give shelter from hot summer days, but mostly the weather is mild and comfortable.

Apart from fishing, I was a birding enthusiast. This area had a rich and varied wild-animal population. Wild life was plentiful and, with little effort, the wartime rationing could be supplemented with a variety of game.

One day, I'd ridden my bicycle to St. Asaph to try locating the nest of a sparrow hawk. On the bridge crossing the River Clwyd leading to the city you could look up the hill leading to the beautiful cathedral. Up there, at the top of the wide Main Street, was the church dedicated to St. Asaph, with its great steeple which seemed to be beckoning believers to pray. I didn't go to church, but I always felt safe and comforted by its presence. To be classified as a city and receiving a city Charter, it must have a cathedral and the ecclesiastical hierarchy which goes along with it. So even though the city of St. Asaph was and is quite small, it is important for its religious influence.

Proceeding along the riverbank, I realized that recent heavy rain had caused the river to become murky. Floating branches made their way along on the tenuous pathway to the sea. Suddenly I noticed what appeared to be an enormous fish floating amongst the debris. The mess was slowly proceeding along. Always alert to take advantage of natural events, it struck me that a fish that size would realize a lot of cash. I ran to the bridge about a hundred yards away and, finding a long pole, I waited until the fish would pass underneath.

There it was, about thirty yards away. Wow, the fish was big. I realized it was a salmon and would weigh probably as much as I could possibly carry. I trimmed the branches and twigs from my pole and as the fish floated by I guided it towards the riverbank. Such an easy task. It disappeared under the bridge and I positioned myself to be able to continue my work when the fish reappeared on the other side. Only a few seconds and once more I could use my stick to guide the fish to the bank.

I retrieved my bike and tried to figure out a way to take the fish into Rhyl where I could sell it. It must weigh 25 to 30 pounds and looked to be about 3 feet long. Grappling with the slimy fish was difficult and the thing kept sliding out of my hands onto the ground. But using the long, grass, to wipe my hands, I eventually was able to secure the huge fish to the crossbar of the bike using the rope which I used to climb trees for bird-nesting.

I headed for Rhyl and, because of my reluctant passenger, I was unable to ride, so the trip to town took most of the afternoon. I noticed the fish now beginning to have a very unpleasant smell. Passing along Wellington Road a lot of people began to show interest in my enormous salmon. I stopped at the "Hugh Jones Garage" and with the water-hose I gave the fish a good wash. I was quite pleased as it smelled much better after its bath. Continuing along the road past the restaurant, the owner came out and asked me if the salmon was for sale. Always keen to take advantage of opportunities I told him it was and I offered it for £5. He asked where I had caught it and I told him in the Clwyd at St. Asaph, but I did not add the detail about it being dead and floating along.

The buyer ran back into the restaurant and came out with £5 and we undid the cord and I helped the man into the store with the fish.

Wow, £5...how pleased my mother would be when I presented her with the money.

I thought about the smell and I wondered if the people would get sick if they were to eat it. Maybe the owner would serve it to his customers in the restaurant and they would die. But I put the thoughts out of my mind and figured that was none of my business, right?

Yes, my mom was very pleased with the windfall, and put the cash to good use. I can tell you that in return I received the best hugs that I ever remember.

•••••

Post script:

Close to St. Asaph is the interesting village of Bodelwydden, famous for its beautiful, white marble church and its quarry. The church holds memories of WWI, where the dead from the close-by Army Base, Kinmel Camp, are buried, victims of the flu epidemic which ravaged the world in the terrible winter of 1918/19.

There in Kinmel Camp, Canadian soldiers waiting for repatriation while frustrated, hungry and cold, rioted to express their anger over their treatment. The last straw was when they learned that Trans Atlantic ships had started carrying tourists to North America while still many war-weary soldiers were waiting to go home.

Pediculosis

I was a small, puny boy when I was thirteen. The war was a year old and it was bitter cold that winter. We lived at number 8, Laurel Dene, Swilly, Plymouth. I attended Plymouth Public High School on Cobourg Street. My memories at that time ranged from dread to peaks of joy. It is hardly credible that a human brain can be the repository of so much information, but I can assure you, that as you age often those obscure memories can be re-lived. Now, why on earth would I think of this episode of my young life? Only to admit to myself that I fought for my rights and won against serious odds

Our toilet was unheated and outside our house like everyone else's in our neighbourhood. It was in effect what many call an outhouse. At that time I had a cold and was in the loo clearing my sinuses using the newspaper strips that my mother provided. Kleenex and more gentle tissue was way off in the future. Over-enthusiasm for the task at hand caused me to blow too hard and my right eardrum ruptured. I don't recall that I cried with the pain, but it was searing and I ran into the house and threw myself into the arms of my mother and begged her to help me.

In this world there is one person who whatever the situation can be relied on for help, love and care and that is your mother. My Mom had a brood of seven at that time and the youngest, Jennifer, was under a year. Mom gathered up the baby, wrapped her in a blanket, took me by the hand and assigning my older sister Grace, to be in charge while she was gone. Off we went by bus, to the Plymouth City Hospital. I have no memory of the bus-ride, however, I do remember we checked in the emergency department of the hospital and I was given a bed in a large, public ward.

I recall that same night a lone enemy plane dropped a bomb on the hospital and it fortunately landed on the far wing and thankfully no-one was harmed.

I remember the nurse put a few drops of warmed, oil in my injured ear which lessened the pain. My mother was sent away and I was bed-ded down for the night, in the luxury of clean sheets. There were about twenty beds in my ward, and they were all occupied. I slept on and off through most of the night and early next morning. I was roused by a large nurse and taken to the doctor's office to have my ear examined. A white-coated man briefly looked in my ear and mumbled some in-structions to the nurse, then left.

A second nurse arrived and I accompanied the two nurses to a near-by room where I was told that I had fleas and would have to have my head shaved. "Shave my head...?" I shouted. "What for?"

The older of the two nurses had a firm grip on my arm and she said in a not unkindly voice, "It's to get rid of the nits and fleas so your brothers and sisters won't get infected."

The other nurse had prepared a basin of evil-smelling chemicals with which to wash my hair and with one holding me firmly, the other approached with her basin. The tools for cutting my hair and shaving my head were nice and handy, beside the sink. All this was happening so quickly, it took only a few seconds to realize the dreadful situation. I could imagine going to school with no hair and the boys making fun of me. With a yell I tore myself loose from the nurse's grip and tried to make my escape. The nurses were both bigger than me but fear gave me strength and I refused to be shorn. We fought for a few minutes while the nurses tried to do their duty.

I held out, and after a few minutes one of the nurses left and the room became quiet and peaceful. The nurse who reminded me of my Mom, put her arm around my shoulder and quietly said, "Maybe there is another way."

Soon the other nurse returned and there was a nice smile on her face. "The doctor says we can use the yellow ointment instead."

Even though I was still unsure what this treatment would entail, obviously it was a reprieve from the dreaded shaved head. Then, in a less confrontational atmosphere, the senior nurse explained that they would first wash out my hair and comb out the pediculosis. Then dry my hair and rub yellow ointment in it, which must remain on my head for twenty four hours. The treatment began at once and I soon realized that these two wonderful ladies had only my best interest at heart. My head was carefully scrubbed, soaped and scrubbed again, and when all the cleaning was done a great slab of gooey, yellow, ointment was rubbed into my scalp. More oil was placed in my ear and I was sent back to my ward.

In the meantime, during the night I had been unable to sleep. The old man in the cot, two over from mine, was gasping for breath and moaning. At about five a.m. he had given a last choking sigh and died. There was quite a to-do with doctors and nurses rushing around. Finally a sheet was pulled up over his face and his cot was pushed out of the ward. The following morning my Mom came to the hospital and took me home.

My ear healed after a few days of the oil treatment and since that time I have never been troubled by fleas.

Phyllis The Donkey Girl

Mr. Jones had a small herd of donkeys that he ran on the western beach of Sunny Rhyl, in Wales. Children would have a ride on a donkey in return for a small fee. Though the donkeys were tame and quite docile, he would put the child on the donkey and holding the animal's bridle he would run with the donkey along the sandy beach, for about a hundred yards.

Sometimes he would take several customers at the same time. He would bring his donkeys onto his pitch about 10 a.m., after first leaving old "Charlie," his big, old, black, donkey with me on the corner, where I did my work. The traffic would stop to allow Mr. Jones to take his herd across the road near the public toilets, in order that he could begin his day's work.

Business was brisk in the donkey-ride trade, and the more money he made, the more he would have to run up and down the beach. Jones was about fifty years of age that year and it struck me that he was doing far too much running, for a man of his age. The Donkey Man was small and thin and not particularly prepossessing. By his own admission, he had a severe case of hemorrhoids. One day, around lunch-time, an ambulance came to the beach, across the road and took Mr. Jones the Donkey man to the Royal Alex Hospital, at the other end of the sea-front.

"I won't go into the nasty details except to say, that finally, his condition, exacerbated by the constant running, had caused his swollen veins to burst."

He lost a lot of blood and suffered a great deal of pain. Typically his stoicism had prevented him from calling out for help. Emergency care, surgery and a few weeks in hospital and Mr. Jones was back on the job. However, in the meantime several young men's hearts had been broken.

In a way, running donkeys was akin to show biz, the show must go on and Phyllis the Donkey girl, the eighteen year-old daughter of the sick man, stepped up to the plate and assumed her father's role. It was the following morning that I met Phyllis for the first time when she brought Charlie to my workplace.

I was stunned at first by the way Jones's replacement looked. She was average height and that was all that was average about her. God, how stunning she was with her long, blond, sun-bleached, hair and skin like a perfect peach even down to that hint of short fuzz. Her lips were full and bowed, her eyes were a startling blue, protected by long, thick, eyelashes which curled in such an attractive manner. Her figure was slender, yet curvy in the right places, she was a picture of perfect health and beauty.

She knew my name and when she was leaving she said "Goodbye and take good care of Charlie."

I was tongue-tied and must have looked a fool gawking after her as she hastened the dozen or so donkeys across the road and on to the beach.

I should explain about Charlie. I rented the donkey, the herd's patriarch at a pound a day, to assist me in my photography business. Charlie was too old to run on the beach so he in a way was semi-retired. I want to tell you about this old friend, so many tales to be told, but those yarns are written elsewhere.

Several times during the course of that day, I crossed the road to see what Phyllis was up to. She was doing exactly what her Dad used to do, but he was never bothered by such a crowd of male admirers, of all ages. Even those handsome, sun-tanned, beach-bums were unable to gain her attention.

After her work was done she brought her charges from the beach, collected Charlie, then she went home. She lived about two miles from her pitch, and it was such a pleasant, musical sound to hear those little, hard, hoof-beats trotting along the pavement. It had been a busy day and the animals knew their way home equally as well as the Jones's.

I knew where the Jones's lived. They had a small pig farm, near the water tower. I would walk that way sometimes to see if I could get a glimpse of her. I did see her once or twice, but she was always so busy either with the donkeys or the pigs.

Each day when I saw her I would ask her to come walking with me, and she always turned me down, I didn't feel too bad as she turned down all the other suitors too, always with such a charming smile.

She would look straight at you, her head tilted and a smile on her perfect lips, her blue eyes semi-closed against the bright sun. It was so incongruous, a girl who was such a "looker" doing that sort of job. It struck me that she could become a movie star. That would have been more appropriate.

She was such a natural sort of person. She replaced her Dad for about six weeks and I don't think she realized it but her beauty tantalized several boys, myself included, for all that time and not once did she date any of us.

Nothing good, or for that matter bad, ever lasts forever. Mr. Jones, the Donkey Man came back on the beach and continued to run the donkeys, his surgery was an obvious success. We all missed seeing that gorgeous, young girl, except in an occasional dream. Everything returned to normal on the beach.

It was a month or so later that we learned that Phyllis had married her Dad's helper at the pig-farm. What a waste, I thought! She could have married me.

My Navy 1945-1946
(How I Remember It)

The last month—early September 1945. My company, British Empire Films, organized a "Welcome Home" fund to celebrate the end of the war and welcome our heroes back.

The idea was to hold entertainments in the castle in Rhuddlan, North Wales, where we would give our thanks to the men who had been the first to return home from the front. The war In the Pacific was still in progress, but the signs were everywhere, that the Pacific War would soon be history. However, I had just received my letter from the Admiralty telling me I was needed.

I joined the Royal Navy on October 2nd, 1945. A car accident caused me to report for duty one day late, and while explaining the circumstances to the reporting officer, his facial expression told me that this event would haunt my stay in His Majesty's Senior Service. In any case, I was eighteen years of age, and though I would have preferred to remain a civilian, this was my duty and I cheerfully swore to serve my country with honor and enthusiasm.

The Royal Navy induction center was located in Butlin's Holiday Camp, Skegness, Yorkshire. The accommodations were reduced to a minimum as far as amenities were concerned. The holiday chalets were crowded with double bunks to accommodate us, the recruits: four to six men to a room. The peacetime swimming pools were empty. The dance hall was now a uniform center, the pubs and other social venues were now doctors' cubicles, dental offices, and classrooms for the purpose of lecturing and psychological testing of we sailors-to-be.

The induction center gave each recruit a personal file and naval ID number. This nine-digit number remains with you for life and I know of men, in the throes of senility, who may not remember the names of their own wife and children, or even their own name, but who remember their military number.

Mine is an easy one: LFX776165. The center conducted medical and dental exams, vaccinations and aptitude testing to determine what work each man would be allocated. The center rigged each man out with two uniforms, one for working and one for best. The mess provided everyone with three meals per day and the only beverage was tea, though it did not taste like the tea from home. It was common knowledge that saltpeter and bromide was put in our tea to diminish our libido, which of course was denied by our leaders.

The last part of our processing was being assigned a posting, a final uniform check and a rail voucher, along with a small amount of money.

I was assigned to HMS Gosling, in Warrington, Lancashire. It took a few days to get used to Navy terminology. Our rooms were "cabins," the dining room "the mess-deck," the doctors office was "the sick bay." Left and right were "port" and starboard." It was confusing, but after just a few days we were playing the game like everyone else. We lined up for our clothing, an NCO would look us up and down, shout some numbers to an assistant, we would receive our uniforms, a personal blanket, a kit-bag and hammock, and a sewing kit which was known as a "Housewife." We were permitted to try on the boots before they were issued. Some of the uniforms fitted fairly well, but alterations could be done for just a few pennies. The medicals didn't take long once they were started. There were no nurses, only sailors who were known as "sick bay attendants." They took our temperatures, weighed and measured us, shouted at us and vaccinated us. Doctors tapped our chests, held our scrotums, looked up our behinds and pronounced us fit. I saw no one fail the medical exam.

The dentist was another matter. After the usual line up I saw a naval dentist who decided I needed one extraction and one filling. He immediately began his professional care. After a while and a lot of pain, I stopped him and asked him if he would mind freezing my jaw.

"Not necessary," he said, "sailors don't feel pain."

"Oh yes they bloody do," I yelled.

He reluctantly gave me an injection and then continued with his work inflicting continued agony. I decided that whatever happened in my life I would never again have dental work done by a naval dentist.

The aptitude and testing took several days. I tried to fit square pegs into round holes, square blocks into circles, tried to listen to dots and dashes over a headset and count the number of each and dealt with pages and pages of questions. I tried to figure out which answer would serve me best.

We were to make our selection of jobs from a long list of vocations from pilots to cooks. I studied the sheet. It was impressive. But how naïve we all were thinking we had a choice. When my turn came I was called into the assignment room, in which I sat in front of a desk behind which were several officers.

"What do you want to be?" asked the head officer.

"Well sir, by trade I'm a photographer and enjoy that job. My second choice would be a physical training instructor, as my hobbies include athletics and long-distance running."

After a short discussion the officer declared that my scores indicated an exceptional aptitude for mechanics. They assigned me to the Air Mechanics (engines) Course. I immediately begged for re-assignment, to no avail.

Later, we boys were taken in a covered truck to the railroad station, where we waited for our trains to different parts of the country, I was bound for Warrington, Lancashire, and arrived there several hours later. I reported to the HMS Gosling only to discover that what was referred to as a ship was in fact a barracks. It was here at HMS Gosling that basic training, more commonly known as "Square-bashing," was completed.

I was one of a class of 24 SUTs. (sailors under training). Our instructor was Leading Seaman Hickock. Our divisional officer was a young man of 19, Sub-Lieutenant Hubbard of Top Division. Our class was accommodated in a large cabin furnished with single narrow cots, each with a foot locker. Our new home was clean and comfortable, the amenities were excellent. We slept well and each morning a seaman entered our sleeping area banging on a dust bin lid with a club and yelling "Heave Ho Le Ho Le Ho Le Ho, Lash up and stow,[1] hands off cocks, on

1 The order "Lash up and stow" refers to the times when ships of the line sailed the seven seas and sailors slept between decks in hammocks which had to be bundled up out of the way when not in use.

socks. Rise and shine, the morning's fine, breakfast in fifteen minutes."
(Or words to that affect.)

We spent a lot of time on the parade ground learning to march, regular and double time, how that would come in handy for an "Air Mechanic (engines)" I can't imagine. We spent a part of each day doing physical exercise. I enjoyed this, as my hobbies included activities which kept me in good physical health. We trained in the use of fire-arms, including the Lee Enfield Rifle, the Sten Gun, Bren Gun and Lewis Gun. On top of the regular training, I joined the Navy Fencing team and was trained in the use of the Sabre, the Epee and the Foil.

However, the Petty Officers who dealt with our parade ground training were brutal. One instance took place when we were in full uniform and carrying our rifles, marching on the parade ground. Our POs. were displeased with our performance and made us double around the parade ground with our rifles above our heads. After about a half hour of this punishment, we stood to attention and were told to remain like that until released. After a while one of the trainees, a tall, skinny lad, passed out and hit his head on the ground. He bled quite a lot and a few comrades ran to help him. Over the P/A a PO screamed "Get Back To Attention." The lad was taken to the sick bay, where a health problem was discovered and he was released on medical grounds. This behavior was to toughen us up, and I must agree that it did. After just a few weeks we became a tough and resilient group.

Lectures were interesting. Eventually we pretended to be ignorant of the most mundane subjects. One instructor began his piece by asking if any of us in class who were animal lovers or farmers. We all kept silent. Then one young lad offered the information that he was a farmer. "Good" said the teacher, "Off you go and clean up the goat's quarters." The goat, our ship's mascot, looked smart in his colorful regalia, but stank like a pole-cat. Our man spent the rest of the morning cleaning up after the goat while we took turns dismantling an old Lewis Gun. Our shipmate joined us later, and you could tell from the stench of him where he had been for the first part of the day.

Another lecture was given on the Lee Enfield rifle. The teacher began by asking if any of us knew anything about the Lee Enfield. One of my high school requirements had been to give a lecture to my class on any subject using flip charts. Because my soldier father told me all about his rifle, I was quite familiar with it. I made the mistake of telling the instructor that I knew something about the rifle, to which he replied, "Alright, you smart assed know-it-all, you come out here and tell us all about it." I took up the challenge and after getting started he told me to sit down and stay quiet.

We each were issued with a Lee Enfield 303, and some days later we were taken to the range for firing practice. That early November morning, the normal Lancashire fog was particularly thick. The visibility was about 30 feet. We were going to shoot targets at 100, 200 and 300 feet. The instructor was in an unusually friendly mood and, gathering us around him in a cluster while waiting for the fog to lift, recounted stories of his experiences.

He then asked, "What is the first thing you do when you get to the firing point?"

There was a little silence, after which I muttered, "gtdhujgd bbevrfdghakjudn."

"What did you say?" he shouted.

"Get out the radar equipment sir," I stated in a quiet voice.

"That man keep quiet or you'll get six lace-holes up your arse," he roared.

Actually it turned out that the instructor was quite a helpful person whose bark was worse than his bite. The fog eventually lifted and we all finished our assignments successfully, even though several missed the targets completely.

We were allowed out of camp on weekends and would present ourselves at the camp guardhouse for inspection. We were always criticized by our POs, but rarely was a man denied shore leave because of his appearance. We'd preen for quite a while in our quarters and check each other for faults before marching to inspection. Quite often, just outside the camp exit, there would be a few ladies hanging about. We had been warned by our POs to have nothing to do with those girls because of the VD.

I was, as were most of the boys, quite innocent on the matter of sex, and I couldn't figure out how our leaders knew they had VD. Anyway, I was never accosted and nor were any of my shipmates. Mind you it would have been a waste of time if the PO had been right, we seldom had more than bus-fare in our pockets. I would take a bus into the city and stroll around. Sometimes I'd pop into the Sally-Ann for a cheap snack. The NAAFI (Navy, Army and Airforce Institute) was another place for a cheap snack. The menu was always the same, tea and a wad, (sweet bun). Often I had no money at all, and at these places nothing was free.

I had been told about another outfit, the FCF (Forces Christian Fellowship). Food there was free. After strutting around downtown for a few hours, I came across a small plaque on a dingy doorway reading " FCF All Welcome." I entered what appeared to be a small dimly lit, musty theatre, maybe 200 seats for an audience. Several elderly ladies wearing aprons were manning a table with a large urn and a stack of cups.

"Is there anything to eat?" I asked.

The reply was "Yes, right after the prayer and the speaker."

I took a seat amongst the eight or so that made up the audience. In a few minutes the preacher came on stage, welcomed us, told us we would sing a few hymns and then have a short talk by a famous doctor, then we would be served tea and buns. We sang the songs and heard the brief sermon, and then the speaker came onto the stage in the company of the FCF vicar, he introduced the guest as Dr. Alexander Fleming, medical scientist and discoverer of Penicillin.

Dr. Fleming seemed so ordinary, youthfully middle-aged and dressed in tweeds. He took one of the chairs that were props and dragged it to center stage by the footlights. In a quiet, dignified voice, he asked the audience to gather around closer as he did not want to shout. By this time we realized that today we were in the company of a man who, with his team of scientists, had saved millions of lives, and we shuffled to be closer to where he sat.

Alexander Fleming—here he was in person, talking to maybe a dozen young sailors. Dr. Fleming gave us a short history of penicillin and told us about his role in its discovery. We were invited to ask questions, but despite his kindly nature we were either too ignorant or awestruck to ask anything. He shook hands with all of us before leaving us to our tea. Can you imagine this man, a national hero, savior of millions, spending an hour in that dismal place, November 1945, with a few lonely sailors and me, LFX776165? He did not stay to have tea with us. I imagine he was needed to help others more in need. But I do recall that as I walked back to base, I walked taller and vowed to be a better man. The memory of that chance occasion still remains vivid.

During our initial training we were given lectures on social diseases—200 trainees about my own age assembled in a hall containing chairs and benches. Around the walls were life-size posters, showing naked men and women in various stages of syphilis and gonorrhea. The medical officer in charge proceeded to lecture us on every aspect of the diseases with many reference to the posters. Two sailors fainted. I can tell you, that lecture put the fear of God into us. The doctor was talking about gonorrhea and was describing the symptoms, the first stage, the second stage, then to wind up the subject, he told us "the third and final stage is lack of feeling in your extremities, you are unable to feel your hands and feet, which become numb." There was a lot of scuffling and scraping of chairs as we began to stamp our feet to see if we had caught something sinister. Following our dismissal, we continued to think this over. I kept clear of females for months, such had been the effects of that awful lecture.

The course of training wasn't all work, even though often we were cursed and abused. There were good times. Our Divisional Officer, Sub-Lieutenant Hubbard came with us on the assault course and games of rugby. It turned out that our "Snotty" was a pretty good type. I had some infraction and had been assigned to polish our Leading Seaman's cabin floor. I was given a can of wax, a toothbrush and a cloth to do the job. Mr Hickock lay on his bunk watching me do the work and telling me how his son was also in the navy. After a while he probably realized the absurdity of one man polishing another's floor using a toothbrush, he told me to stop and go and have some fun. After that incident I saw our Kilick (Leading Seaman) in a different light.

I was very friendly with our physical training instructor in charge of fencing. I suggested we put on a bit of a show for the boys. The PTI, a perfect specimen of a healthy man, was about 21. He agreed with the plan. As I recall there are seven guard positions when fencing with the sabre; one is the *en guarde* position and the others for protecting six areas of the body. During rehearsal of our "duel," we would whisper the guard position of the next attack. Of course, the opponent would be in a good position to protect himself when the attack came. We rehearsed the show, and one evening when the gym was crowded we began our fake match. The system was great. We fought for several minutes before a crowd of about 200 cheering sailors. My, that was good fun.

Eating our meals was something else. We each carried our own cutlery, known as "shooting irons," and a mug. We were assigned ten to a table. A kitchen worker would supply each table with ten portions of each course and ten plates. It was the responsibility of the two men at the end of the table to share the food. The system sounds good in theory, but in practice the two men at the end took a lions-share before passing the food along and often the last to be served got very little. An officer routinely came around the mass-deck calling "Any Complaints?" Of course there weren't any. The officer had the habit of hitting his leather knee-length boots with his swagger stick, and always had a scowl on his face. After dinner we would be off to the NAAFI cafeteria for a cup of tea and a wad.

I was sent to do kitchen duties for one day. I peeled potatoes mostly. I also washed dishes and mopped the floor (deck). I watched the cooks making fruit cakes for our desserts. What I thought were raisins in the cake turned out to be cockroaches, which fled from the ovens in droves before the cooks slammed the oven doors shut. I was turned off desserts for ages after seeing that. But otherwise the food, though bland, was quite edible.

All good things come to an end. We graduated from boot camp and were shipped off to South Wales. We reported to HMS Gileston which in reality was Wing #4 of the Royal Air Force base and 32nd maintenance unit, St Athen's. It was at this station that our Air Mechanics (engines) training would take place and would be our home for the next six months.

St. Athen's must have been one of the biggest military camps in the UK at that time. Wing #4, the Royal Navy training section, housed several hundred navy personnel at its peak. As each class graduated and were posted, a new group of about the same size were inducted; however, by far the majority at the base were RAF personnel and perhaps a thousand civilian workers.

The mess-deck, wing #4, was enormous, and nearly 400 personnel could sit down to eat at the same time. The method of serving was quite different than at HMS Gosling. Here there were serving lines manned by kitchen staff. Large steam tables kept the food hot. We sailors lined up and quickly went past the servers and received our food. It was amazing how quickly so many men could be served. Our dinner was usually potatoes, vegetables and a meat dish, dessert and two slices of dry bread. We carried our own cutlery and mug, and helped ourselves to tea from an enormous urn. It was our responsibility to return our dishes to the servery when finished. In general, the food was good and sufficient. Tea and water were the only beverages available; milk, coffee, soft drinks or juices were just not available. At St. Athens we were never asked if we had any complaints.

Following breakfast each weekday morning dressed in our coveralls, carrying our cutlery and mugs in our left hands, we were marched from our wing to the hangars where our training took place. An Able Seaman was in charge of us during this one-mile march. I don't recall his name, he was a cockney and he took every opportunity to curse and abuse us, I have no idea what motivated his behavior but as time went on his foul abuse became very personal and included references to our mothers which were not complimentary. One Monday morning we were assigned a different in-charge. We later discovered that following an evening of drinking in a local pub, while staggering back to base, he had been set upon by a group of trainees who avenged themselves of his abuse by giving him a beating and throwing him into an outgrowth of noxious weeds. When he recovered he was transferred. We were very pleased.

Our instructors were civilians and were experts in their profession. The officer in charge of the training program was Lt. Commander Ireland. Our first week's training was in the use of metal files. We were given a piece of mild steel and, with a file and hacksaw, we were to produce a finished piece measuring 2x2 ½ inches. This seemingly simple task was probably one of the most difficult projects I have ever done. What this taught us was patience and exactitude, qualities lacking in most teenagers, but necessary when working with aircraft engines.

Sixteen redundant pilots had been assigned to our training division. These men were two or three years older than the rest of us. All of the pilots were Canadians who had voluntarily joined the Fleet Air Arm and had undergone extensive training, had graduated as Navy Pilots. After being given their wings they had been declared redundant. They were a bright and handsome group of young men who were being remustered as Mechanics. They were most disgruntled when their valuable skills were no longer required by the Navy. They let it be known that none of them intended to pass the course but wanted to be released and returned home to Canada. Ultimately all purposely failed their mechanic exams, but rather than be sent home, they were re-assigned as cooks, much to their dismay.

One incident took place that involved our Canadian friends. Church Parade was compulsory then, and we were compelled to meet after breakfast every Sunday wearing our Number Ones. We were marched to the Camp Theater where Church Service was held. Outside the theater the order " Catholics and Jews, fall out" was given and the rest of us took our places in the audience seats. Our Padre was a Lt. Commander and he and the rest of the commissioned Officers sat on the stage. Each exit was manned by NCOs wearing webbing and side-arms. The service got under way. The captain made a short speech in which he criticized us for being dirty and unkempt. Then the padre gave a sermon which was most un-Christian. He filled in the details of the captain's generalized comments. At the point in his harangue, where he called us dirty pigs, one of the Canadians jumped out of his seat and loudly declared, "I'm not listening to this crap." The rest of his pals did the same. Suddenly the Padre screamed out, "Mutiny, Mutiny" and the response was that the POs at the doors drew their side-arms and adopted a threatening stance. There was a lot of milling about and for a while the tension was frightening. After a while, things quieted down and the service came to an end and we were all dismissed.

In any group there are troublemakers. One morning while we were marching to work we were passing the Yard-Arm, which was usually flying the Union Jack and the Navy Pennant. This day someone had attached a bunch of inflated condoms to the flagpole. When we noticed this we broke into screams of laughter and started to salute the flag. It took a few minutes for our NCO to quiet us down and to continue on our way. Later that afternoon, the entire Wing #4 was paraded, and the officers tried to find the culprit. Not one admitted fault so we were all confined to base pending finding who was responsible. There were about 5,000 RAF on the base, and as the likelihood of the culprit being one of us was quite remote, the matter was dropped.

A couple of days later, we were paraded in our Number Ones and marched off to the far side of the parade ground. We were advised that the purpose was an FFI (Free from infection) Inspection. We asked what that was. "You'll find out soon enough," we were told. We came to a secluded part of the parade ground and ordered to lower our trousers while the officers and the Navy Doctor walked up and down our ranks examining our private parts for signs of STD, then we were instructed to get dressed then dismissed. The navy doctor that day was a lieutenant who happened to be a woman. I find this event almost unbelievable even though I was there.

Each morning we were marched to the hangars, where we were instructed in aircraft engine maintenance. Our first airplane being the De Havilland Tiger Moth with its Gypsy Major engine, under the guidance of the instructor we removed the engine and dismantled it, spreading the hundreds of parts on the work-bench. Our objective was to get to know what each part looked like and then clean and re-assemble the whole thing. All this was done under the keen scrutiny of our instructor.

We were asked to name the engine parts. "What's that called?" the instructor asked.

"A connecting rod sir," I replied.

"What does it do?" he asked.

"A connecting rod is a mechanical device for converting a reciprocal motion to a rotary motion." I had learned well and was able to satisfy the leader with my reply.

We were enthusiastic about learning the mysteries of how a motor worked. Eventually we got all the pieces back together and managed to get the Gypsy installed back in the Tiger's airframe. After connecting all the controls, with no bits left behind, we felt rather proud of ourselves.

Our joy dampened a bit when the instructor then said, "Now for the moment of truth... start the motor on the first try." He sat in the cockpit and gave us our instructions. "It takes two to start the engine, one in the cockpit and one to swing the propeller. You Trower, you know the routine, you'll go first. Stand facing the prop and with your right hand gripping the trailing edge of the prop, when you are ready you will tell the pilot 'Switches Off.' The pilot will confirm 'Switches Off'. You then want to prime the engine so your next call is 'Petrol On.' Petrol on is confirmed. Then call 'Suck In' and you slowly turn over the engine to prime the cylinders. A couple of turns should be about right."

I carefully followed the instructions hardly daring to breathe.

"Set the prop at an angle where you can hold it to give a good swing, when you are ready call 'Switches On.' The pilot will reply 'Switches On.' When he calls 'Contact,' at that moment you with your feet a short pace apart, give the propeller a good swing and follow through by walking to the side of the plane. You never want to be in front of a turning propeller if you want to live."

Imagine my surprise and joy when the engine coughed into life and with a cloud of smoke disappearing into the slipstream, the motor was alive and ticking over beautifully. Our class gave a loud cheer. The engine was shut down in a few minutes and every trainee had to take a turn.

Naturally, we were jubilant at our success with the Tiger Moth. It meant we could proceed to the next phase of our study, the Rolls Royce Merlin, which was the power plant used in many operating war-planes. We were to become familiar with the Merlin's engines and the carburetors, supercharger, variable pitch propeller, fuel tanks, instruments etc. Also we were instructed on the maintenance of the Hercules engine, which was a huge radial sleeve-valve motor, which thankfully we were never called on to work with.

Next, we were marched to another hangar, where we were shown the biggest and most powerful of military piston engines, the American Pratt and Whitney 36 Cylinder radial. And what was referred to as a secret weapon was in the back of a truck. Someone peeled back the tarpaulin and exposed a Rolls Royce Nene Jet Engine, there had been whispers about that jet motor and today we were to have it demonstrated.

"You men," the instructor called out, "this is not for general knowledge. You must keep quiet about what you are going to see."

Someone started the jet and the thing burst into life with a strange whining roar. We could see the hot, compressed air being blasted out of the tail pipe and smell the burning kerosene.

All the while we were lectured on its power and successes. Finally, to demonstrate its awful power, an iron bar, held by several sailors at each end, was carried into the jet-blast and the bar actually started to

bend with the force of the jet. Then the engine was shut down and covered and carefully hidden from any possible prying eyes.

About half way through the course I received a message from home
to the effect that my mother had had an accident and had hurt her arm
in a motor car accident. I applied for a leave to go home to see my
mother and my request was denied. Being without cash for the train
fare, I sold my personal blanket to an Italian prisoner of war[2] and left
for home. I stayed home with my mom for three days and was planning
on returning to base when two naval police came to my home. I was
out at the time and my mother refused to tell them where I was. I cut
short my stay and took the next train back to St. Athens. Reporting for
duty, I was arrested for being AWOL. The following day I was marched
into the Captain's office and found guilty, but before I could be sen-
tenced the Captain turned purple and had to be taken to the sick bay.

The following day, the second-in-command, a Squadron Leader
Aitkin, gave me my punishment. "Well son," he said quietly, "you did
wrong and should not have gone AWOL. I realize your mother was
hurt but that is no excuse. I punish you to the minimum I am allowed
to sentence you, six days in the brig."

"Thank you, sir," I said and was hustled off to serve my sentence.
The next few days went pleasantly enough. The head jailer was a neighbor from my town. He treated me well, gave me all the food I wanted
and all I had to do was to keep my cell clean. It took me a while to get
used to my bed, which was three planks of wood with a piece of shaped
wood for a pillow. When released, I resumed my training and nothing
more was said about the affair.

While at St. Athens we were able to use the camp gymnasium. I
spent most of my free time there, doing weight-lifting, sword-fencing
and gymnastics. The officers in charge of the gym were all Air Force
and didn't seem to show any superior attitude towards enlisted men.
After a while I used to take a turn looking after the gym while the duty
officer was relaxing in the officer's mess. Strange though, not many
used the gym even though the camp population was in the vicinity of

2 There were many Italian prisoners of war in this area, working on local farms or working as helpers in the military kitchens. Most would be soon sent home when the Pacific war
was over. These men lived comfortably and moved about without let or hindrance, many had
married local girls and never did return to Italy. It was an irony to learn that these men were
provided with hot water for their ablutions and sheets for their beds, we sailors enjoyed neither
of these comforts.

5,000 men and women. An interesting airman I made friends with was a bit strange. He was about twenty and from Manchester, a tailor by trade. In his uniform he looked quite a stocky man, always looked a little disheveled. Stripped for his weight work-out he was a mass of powerful developed muscle and very strong. He was seen often sitting on roadside and when asked he claimed he had forgotten where he lived, he confided in me that he was working on being dismissed from the service on account of mental deficiency. He played other tricks too and eventually he was released and sent home to Manchester.

There was one sad incident at Wing #4, The trainee two cots to my left in our mess was a bit of a loner. He was quite tall and had a squint. There had been several complaints made to our NCO, that small personal items had gone missing. Items such as watches, pens, rings, etc. One man reported that a writing set given to him by his mother had disappeared. The ship's Master at Arms along with other officers conducted a search of our foot-lockers. When opening our friend's locker he began to cry, great sobs came from his throat when in his locker was found the missing things. He was arrested right away and taken to the guard-house. The following Monday the boy was tried for theft.

To prepare for the court marshal, a stage had been constructed in a vacant grassy area of the camp. Seats were placed on the stage for the officers. The order was given that all ratings were to attend the trial in Number One uniforms. The man was marched in with an armed petty officer on each side of him. The sailor was not allowed to wear his hat and his sobbing was heard by the entire ships company. The trial was brief, the crime details were given. "Guilty or Not Guilty?" called the senior officer. Between his sobs, he responded "Guilty." The punishment was handed down, one hundred and eighty days in the detention center in Portsmouth.

The man was led off and the assembly was dismissed. No one represented this unfortunate man. I imagine this was navy justice, obviously the lad had some psychological disorder, but justice must be seen to be done. That was the last we saw of the guilty man. Whether he appealed the punishment I have no idea. But we all felt deeply that his punishment did not fit the crime.

In our free time, we could take a train ride to Barry or Cardiff, and locally there were a lot of interesting places to spend some time. I was fascinated with the castle near Llantwit Major, a short bus ride from camp. There was what today is known as Atlantic College. Back then during and for a few years after the war, the army had taken over the castle as a military base. The place was called St, Donat's Castle[3] - and what a magnificent place that was. From the castle main building to the shore of the Severn River, the gardens swept down in tiers, ornamentally landscaped. Starting at the top, a lawn, then a rose garden, one level was decorated with several example of topiary. Further down a small hedge-maze and at the lowest level a large swimming pool. Several of us walked along the beach where the sea had eroded the shale cliffs, and many fossils were lying on the beach and protruding from the cliff face. We collected some of these relics as souvenirs of a beautiful place.

In the village of LLantwit Major is another lovely spot for quiet contemplation: the church of St. Illtyd, said to be the oldest Christian church in the UK. Apparently the original wooden structure burnt down hundreds of years ago and the present stone church was erected. The floor of the church is paved with gravestones hundreds of years old and the vicar who showed us around the church told us that a secret tunnel led to the monastery located some distance away. Well what wonderful adventures young sailors-under-training can have, at the expense of Our Majesty's Government, if they only try.

But of course we were not there for fun, we were training to keep airplanes flying, and soon our course would be completed. We studied hard and tried our best. I was fortunate in that I was able to graduate with high marks and get to sew a badge on my uniform sleeve indicating that I was now an Air Mechanic (Engines) FC.

The badge may have been sewn on a little bit skewed, but my pride was straight and sure. I was one of a group of graduating Air Mechanics who were sent to the Royal Naval Air Service base at Lee-on-Solent. Unfortunately, the skills learned were not to be put to use, following a family crisis where I was needed at home, the authorities released me to the Navy reserve for an indefinite period and I was no longer needed as an air mechanic first class.

3 St. Donat's Castle was purchased in the 1920s by the American newspaper magnate William Randolph Hearst. Mr. Hearst had had the place refurbished for himself and his friends. It was apparent that a great deal of money had been spent as the condition of the castle was magnificent. We were told that Mr. Hearst did come from his Californian home to visit and entertained many high level politicians and other famous people

Tony Blencowe
(A Lancaster is Missing)

I was telling my friend about some interesting men and women I have known, who have since passed away. How was it that in so many cases they were heroes, though they seldom shared their experiences? It was as if a segment of their lives had come to an end. A door had opened, passing through that door was a fresh slate in which they could continue to write their history.

In the case of Tony, he spent most of his time during World War Two in the Royal Air Force. His military service started in 1942 when at the age of nineteen, he volunteered for air crew. After waiting for medical examinations, psychological and aptitude testing, he was sent to the Number Two Initial Training Wing. He was then enrolled in St John's College, at Cambridge University, to do the standard three months of basic training. All military enlistees, volunteer or conscript, Navy, Air Force or Army, were given this short, three month indoctrination. More commonly that period was known as "square-bashing." As that name implies, much of the time was spent drilling on the parade ground. Following the basic training, he was sent to Canada to begin his pilot's training.

With others in the group, indeed as with so many pilots in training, the first airplane model in which Tony was trained on was the famous De Havilland Tiger Moth, complete with its Gypsy Major engine. Western Canada was perhaps the most important aviation training area. Canada was hosting the British Commonwealth Air Training Plan and our country was known as the "Aerodrome of Democracy." This system produced thousands of military pilots and all other types of air crew who were then shipped off to England to fight in the war. Tony did not receive his pilot wings but continued his training as a Navigator and Air Bomber. He finally got his wings as an "Air-Bomber."

Returning to England, Tony continued his training and teamed up with the crew that he would train, live and fight with, until that fateful night that was yet to come. Night and day flying, high and low level navigating, and honing his skills at aiming bombs until those skills became instinctive. Many hours were spent over the skies of Britain through fair and foul weather. Majority of this flying was done on the work-horse of the Air Force, the multi-engine training, done on the Anson. Then earning the rank of Sergeant he was assigned to a fighting squadron of Lancaster Bombers, that's where the real work of war was accomplished. His duties were to be a member of the crew of Air-Bombers trained to attack the Reich.

Most of us imagine that an Air-Bomber (Bomb Aimer) aims bombs and that is the end of our knowledge. In times of war when battles were fought with cannon, the skill of the "Bombardier" more than any other officer, won the day. Today, the pilot is the hero and usually the rest of the crew is an addendum in the aircraft log. In WW Two when those bombing missions took place, the bomb-aimer would perform his duty, lying prone in the very nose of the plane. He was just inches behind the Pers

pex nose-cone through which he would calculate the moment when the aircraft speed, direction and altitude were in conjunction with the target and relay "Bombs Gone" to the pilot. It was at this point in the raid that the many hours of training were to pay off.

For those final minutes leading up to the bombing, he would be in effect piloting the plane. At the same time while staring intently into the bombsight, in temporary control of the aircraft. He would be making small adjustment to direction and speed, then releasing his bombs on to the target. Often, he would be lying for hours in almost total silence (the chatter on the intercom would be pure Hollywood). Cramped in his tiny space, at 20,000 feet or more, with little relief from his sheep-skin flying suit. Enduring the bitter cold, breathing the airplane's supply of oxygen, to sustain his life. With the bomb load spent, the pilot would resume control and make all haste to get back to base. Many times he was beset from all sides and below from enemy gunfire and fighter attack.

Many of these brave young men did not arrive home to their loved ones. Some parachuted to some sort of safety when their plane was destroyed. Extra-ordinary tales of heroism are recorded and many recognized by honors and awards. Look around during November Remembrance Day services and notice how many old men and women bring out their medals or ribbons of honor. Once more they proudly wear them on their chests with pride. Peel back the years if you can and see the youthful, smooth skin and strong, handsome bodies of those heroes. We see expressed in tears our gratitude, our thanks to those who protected our freedom and through those tears we bow our heads and never forget that we are free because of them.

Tony joined the RAF at the age of nineteen, many boys in those war-torn days lied about their age, in order to enlist. Like so many young men he wanted to be a pilot, and be a hero. Instilled with the love of country, the very idea of German boots treading his cherished England roused his anger. As soon as he was able, he applied to join the Air Force and was accepted. He was of average height, slight build and pale skin. He held himself erect, an eager expression in his eyes and was always ready with a quip and a smile. He was always willing to express his opinion, when asked. I recall him many years later, as leader of an Air Training Cadet Squadron, to which my son Terrence belonged.

Tony would urge the cadets to hurry by calling out, "Fill your boots you men" in a loud and incisive voice. That brought back the memory of my early days in the forties, when I was a boy in the A.T.C. Squadron number thirteen forty, in Rhyl, North Wales. I was a recipient of the same command.

"Yes," I got a gong for that, mind you I'd rather it not have happened, I still have recurring nightmares about that trip," he admitted to me.

How those men would deny their bravery. But just look at their chests, there you can see the flags of unspoken heroism. Those medals brought out once each year when those terrifying memories can be recalled. And again hot tears as they remember their fallen comrades. Even the foe welcomed our forces, on that final march to end the war. Though the flowers, smiles and tears were for the army, we all knew that the thanks were for all the victors whether on land, sea or in the air.

We have a sense of joy and happiness when our personal heroes sur-

vive those bitter times, when they once again come home and are re-
united with their waiting families. It's with great sadness and sympathy
that goes out to those whose warriors who did not return home. We
see mothers at the cenotaph every November holding their dead son's
medals, as tears flow down their faces. Again we thank God for the
return of our son or husband. Tony was just twenty one when he made
his final trip to Germany. He did make it home but was to experience
sufficient fear to last him for the remainder of his life.

That fateful day, February second, 1945, during a routine operation
with Karlsruhe as the target, their Lancaster Bomber call sign CA-F,
crashed near the little town of Jarney, France. There was very little
news about the crash and it was only much later that the details were
fully explained by Tony, the only one of the crew to survive.

"Yes, we were on our way home. There were hundreds of our planes
raiding or returning, when all of a sudden there was a loud crash and
the plane started to spin out of control. We began to fall out of the sky.
It was apparent that our right wing for some reason had been chopped.
There was little flak happening at that moment. It became obvious
to me that an airplane flying above us had dropped their bomb-load
and by some fluke of a chance we were below in the way of one of his
bombs. The bomb had struck our starboard wing and we were totally
out of control, spinning out of the sky to disaster. I was pinned against
the nose-cone, and unable to move as the centrifugal force kept me
glued to that area."

"Suddenly, our crippled plane began to disintegrate and the front
of the plane with me attached parted from the main fuselage. I found
myself free falling in the darkness. I didn't know where I was but some
sense of second nature, or it was my training, found my hand on the release handle of my parachute, on my chest. I pulled the handle and the
noise of the rushing air suddenly slowed, as my chute deployed. Horrified, I continued my descent and landed, hurt and shocked in a field.
I returned to consciousness with a very painful hip. My first thought
after checking myself for other injuries was to bury my parachute, as it
might be seen by one of the enemy. No small task in February's frozen
ground, without a shovel!"

"My next thought was to find my crew. The broken Lancaster was
nearby and all of the crew were dead, some horribly disfigured. I laid

out my friends as best I could, most of whom I had spent every moment of the last nine months with. To hide a few miles away was my next thought, until some of my injuries felt better. In the distance I could still hear gunfire and I assumed the enemy were not that far away."

"The following day I encountered some Free French and they fed me and looked after my wounds. After giving me directions, I continued on my way and ran into some American soldiers. They helped me and gave me a lift to a Belgian airport. On February eighth, I was able to get a lift on a Dakota flight leaving for Ardney, England. Then, with a lift on a RAF Lancaster I was on my way back to my base in Skelingthorpe. I reported back on duty. After the shortest of medical examinations and a few days' rest, I was assigned to be a member of the crew of Flight Lieutenant Seddon, on Lancaster CA-D. We were scheduled to do some flight testing and training and from February the twenty fourth until March twenty third, we were flying on a regular basis. Essen, Dortmund, Lutzkendorf and Wesel were among our targets."

There, in a few words are recorded a period of Hell on Earth. How is it possible that in a civilized and enlightened society, this sort of thing can take place, and multiplied a million times?

Tony's memory is still vivid to all who knew him, though few are familiar with this story. We remember him as he was, as a supervisor in the airline, where he was to spend the next thirty years. He was known as an honest and caring man who expected his subordinates to do a decent days' work. Maybe it was part of the military experience, however, he always made his expectations clear and reasonable. He and his fellow employees at the company got along well. Few of his contemporaries are here now, and I am happy to be able to record this moment in his long and exciting career, though I too have reached the age of seniority.

Tony passed away a few years ago leaving behind his loving wife Loretta and two fine sons both of whom are career officers in the Canadian Military.

Bombs Away Wally

Some people are natural-born raconteurs, and others can bore you almost to sleep. A few are able to bring to life vivid scenes of exciting events. It is my fervent hope that the story-tellers you have known are the latter type.

My friend Wally Ford died a few years ago, but man could he tell a thrilling yarn. However, repetition seemed to take the edge off. I recall some of his stories and can still feel their thrill. The story he told me of that unpleasant incident on Canada's West Coast, during the war, I will relate to you. Be mindful that my tale is working from the memory of what he told me. So please understand, the almost impossible task of adding the original humor and fear to the tale, as well as hoping I'm not losing some of the pertinent details.

Wally worked for the Airline. He was a foreman, licensed mechanic. He was an honest man. Before his airline employment he was in the Canadian Air Force. He was a trainee mechanic when the war broke out in 1939. At seventeen he joined the RCAF as a mechanic and soon became a Flight Engineer. His rank when he was de-mobbed in 1946 was that of Warrant Officer. Wally spent a lot of his war-time service as a crew-member in the Four-engine Liberator. Even to the non-experienced individual, it can be assumed that life aboard the operational large bomber could be hazardous.

I would listen to his stories and often it would go through my mind that the story was exaggerated or twisted, for effect. That proved not to be the case as one time in Florida, at the Clearwater Airport we were together, when a Liberator was on display to the public.

To the best of my memory the year was 1995. My friend became quite agitated and insisted on going aboard. The expression on his face was ashen, as if he had seen a ghost. His face was pale and his hands were shaking as he climbed the ladder to enter the plane.

I followed my friend closely, he turned to me as we entered the plane's fuselage.

"I flew this plane," he muttered. Stowed in the cockpit was the air-craft's log-book, he took the book from its stowage. "This is my old airplane," he cried as he leafed back through the old log book. It was indeed his plane as he flipped back through the old faded pages that bore his name, Warrant Officer Walter Ford, flight engineer. That entry was March, 1944. It revealed the flight to be a nine-hour hunt for sub-marines off the coast of Canada.

I lost Wally as he introduced himself to those men who were acting as docents. Those old veterans who were always eager to regale the tourists, with their stories. Now, like a long-lost brother, my friend had joined them in their reminisces. I waited for Wally for two hours in the snack-bar, while he visited with those old airmen. He eventually came to meet me, his face was flushed and youthful and still excited, after exchanging yarns with those old heroes.

We ordered more coffee, my friend went on and on about the old days. I began to wish I was some other place away from my garrulous friend. He abruptly stopped, and looked at me across the table.

With a quizzical slight smile on his face he said, "Trev, did I ever tell you about the time we nearly blew ourselves up on a B24 just like this one?" Well, a story was on its way and even if I was to drop dead it would continue to its last jolt. There was no need for me to respond.

"Yes, that was the time we operated the Liberator, out of Vancouver Airport, the skipper was Old Alan Boyko, from Edmonton. He was a full lieutenant. I flew with him many times and we became good friends. On that particular flight, we had loaded up twenty one-hundred pound bombs, in our main bomb-bay and we flew off to search for Japanese submarines.

"We had set the bomb fuses for contact fire and were barreling down the runway and just as we started our lift-off, we had an engine fire warning, on number three engine. It was daylight and a glance out the window on the starboard side revealed smoke and flames shooting out from the number three engine. As the flight Engineer I sat on the right side of the pilot's seat.

"I was not trained as a pilot but for short periods I would take over the controls while the skipper had a rest or relieved himself. Well Trev, it was not a big deal. We shut down the engine, feathered the prop and shut off the fuel supply to number three engine. Then we fired the extinguisher and put the fire out. The crisis was over, it took about a minute or so.

"The big problem was that we had to scrap the operation, as to be operational we had to have four, good engines. We climbed to eight thousand feet, and out over the Pacific that's where we jettisoned the fuel. We had gassed up for a ten hour flight and were much too heavy to land fully fueled. We could have driven our cars for years on the fuel we dumped. So here we were with a load of armed bombs, approaching Vancouver Airport on three engines. Fortunately, the weather was very favorable.

"Another snag was the fact that we would have to dump our bombs, in order to make a safe landing. The safest place to unload live bombs was in the ocean, where they would do no harm. We approached the airport and lined up with the runway and began a long, slow approach and at the same time we had to jettison our bombs.

"When things go wrong they seem to really go terribly wrong. The bomb-bay door became stuck. Now, it was my job to go back to the area, with the stuck door and pry it open for each bomb that we were releasing.

"There was no radio communication with the pilot flying the plane, so a system was established where the skipper would shout, "Number one bomb is ready."

"I would yell in reply, "Door Open."

"Then he would shout, "Number one bomb away."

"In preparation for the second bomb to be dropped, I would pry open the door in readiness for the number two bomb, and the drill would be repeated.

"All the while this procedure was ongoing, we were gradually approaching our landing position, where we would have disposed of our bomb-load. Then, we planned to make a controlled landing on three engines. After the first few bombs were disposed of safely, we had really gotten into the swing of things. Even over the noise of the engines, I suppose command and responses were unclear. By the time the nineteenth bomb had gone we were no longer really hearing each other.

"We were going through the motions but everything was so simple and straight-forward. And then at about five hundred feet when the last bomb would soon be gone, and fuel was at a minimum. We were committed to land, damn me but didn't the last bomb stick in the doorway and I could not get the thing to drop. I was scared stiff, practically sitting side ways on a live hundred pound bomb sticking half-way out the bomb-bay door. This was happening just as we crossed the shore-line where the runway began.

"I shouted to the pilot, "Go around again." Unfortunately, he could no longer hear me. He was busy on his own, handling the radio and the landing procedures. I was terrified, and thinking, "What if he makes a heavy landing and the bomb shakes loose? We would all be killed."

"I was a wreck, as scary thoughts were swirling through my anxious mind as we approached the last few yards. And there, out of the half-open door I could see the runway ten feet away, eight feet, a mere five feet away. Then, clenching my teeth with a prayer on my lips I heard the squeal of the tires, on concrete and the bomb was still secure. I thanked God for a smooth landing with a skilled pilot. We taxied to a safe place away from the hangar. We gave our report to corporal armourer who met the plane and he quickly reset our wayward bomb on "Safe."

"We still talk about the wild times when we flew, during those years. Today, here we are, old men, and yet a word, a slight smell or some subtle cue and we are transported again to days of our youth, reliving those horrifying war stories."

Aberystwyth – 1947

I had worked for British Empire Films part and full-time since the age of fifteen. I became proficient with all departments of the company, from processing the film, maintaining the photo lab and developing, printing and in selling. Where I excelled was in operating the big 35 mm. movie camera which we used on the Rhyl promenade taking "walking pictures." I seem to have had the knack of obtaining the attention of the passers-by and having them pose for pictures. By working seven days a week, long hours and expending maximum energy I made very good money.

At the peak of the holiday season I could take over a thousand pictures a day and over eighty per cent of the shots were purchased by satisfied customers. Mr. Hobson, the owner of the company, had promised me that once I had completed my National Service, he would be making me a junior partner in the company. When I was released from the Royal Navy, I approached Mr. Hobson regarding the partnership. He explained that he wanted me to run his company in Aberystwyth, West Wales and if I did a good job, next year he would reward me with a junior partnership. So in 1947, at twenty years of age, I proceeded to Aberystwyth and took charge of the business at that location. Besides being the cameraman, I also supervised the photo-lab. The sales department was in the capable hands of Mrs. Mary Clayton.

Aberystwyth, West Wales, is a coastal university and resort town. The sea-front is in the shape of a horse-shoe, stretching from the pier in the south-west to the popular spot known as Constitution Hill to the north-east. This delightful Bay is perhaps one mile from end to end. The beach was pebbled and when the sea was calm the sound of the water curling onto the pebbles, made a lovely, gentle, whispering sound. Pleasure boats would operate from the beach taking people out for cruises or fishing trips.

There was a lot happening in that delightful town, strolling the promenade and beaches, movies, dances, swimming and fishing off the pier. There were amusement arcades, the summer theatre and orchestra or just simply relaxing and doing nothing at all. Beyond the pier was the ruins of Aberystwyth Castle. It was now utilized as a Park, with plenty of seating and the grass was kept trimmed and clean. What a lovely, romantic setting.

There were many tourists visiting this town, some were from England however, it appeared to me that most hailed from other parts of Wales. Thousand of visitors came for day trips, week-ends or otherwise. All in all, business was very good and everyone seemed to do well. This time of the year was generally sunny and mild to warm and the breeze off the sea smelled delightfully fresh. We had our photo-lab in a back street near the pier. For a few days, as I entered the workshop, I was pleasantly surprised by loud, wolf-whistles coming from the house across the lane. I admit that I felt that some shy admirer was hiding while making those sounds. Imagine my disappointment when I discovered that the whistles were coming from a middle-aged, African, grey parrot! Later, when that parrot and I became better acquainted I was amazed at its vocabulary in English and in Welsh.

Business was good and on a personal level, I made many friends and enjoyed my twentieth summer. Even though this town's tourist business was only a fraction of Rhyl's and many other major resorts. I happened to be the only photographer working in Aberystwyth. As a result, all of the business available was conducted by our company. I returned to our main company centre in the early fall and received Mr. Hobson's congratulations, thanks and was given a bonus. Overall, the season was a great success. It was also highlighted by an unusual event which took place during August of that summer.

My friend and I had decided to take a walk up the Constitution Hill. It was a still and clear evening, perfect to just sit and enjoy the stars. We knew that nearly a thousand Welsh coal miners were in town for a week-end of rest and relaxation and this Saturday were gathering at the sea-front for an evening of song. A well known choral conductor had arrived in town and had organized these men for a performance of excerpts from Handel's *Messiah* and other popular, vocal music. It's a well known fact that when Welshmen get together and the circumstances are right, the most beautiful choral music in the world is forthcoming. Adding to the natural ability and heritage of Welshmen, a famous and skillful choirmaster, as well as an outdoor, natural amphitheater, it was anticipated that a pleasant evening was forthcoming.

The weather couldn't have been better; I was in wonderful company, dusk was quietly falling. At about eight p.m., the miners began gathering on the promenade, just to the west of the summer theatre. Its uncanny how that many men were able to organize themselves as several hundred of them were arriving to sing. A small stage had been set up backing onto the beach, upon which the choirmaster would direct their voices. The music began and what ultimate beauty of those men's voices, you'd swear they had rehearsed for months! We were on the hill nearly a half mile away from the stage and we could hear every word quite clearly. A young girl, a soprano, had joined the choir leader on the stage and added her lovely voice to the throng. She sang several arias and her final song *"Oh my Beloved Father,"* brought tears to the eyes of the audience and singers alike.

As darkness fell and the stars came out and the moon cast its silvery glow, the music came to its conclusion. The evening ended as a multitude of voices now sang *"Land of Our Fathers,"* the Welsh National Anthem, and the crowd dispersed. This was more than seventy years ago and when I think of the experience, it is with the most vivid and warm nostalgia. I was there with a lady, Pauline. While listening to the concert, she lay her head on my shoulder and closed her eyes. What lovely feelings of warmth and caring…I didn't move, wanting to keep that moment for always.

Sometime later I was recounting this episode of my life to a friend and could not help adding other details of my time in Aberyswyth that year. The Summer Theater was close, so I would set up my camera to take pictures of the passers-by. The Summer Theater Orchestra was a first class group of musicians who were contracted to entertain tourists. Around the stage there was an open-air theater of about 200 seats. For a very small admittance fee, maybe a shilling or two, you could sit and listen to light, classical music for a couple of hours, in comparative comfort. People not wishing to pay could gather round about the theater and by either standing or sitting, providing they brought along their personal chairs, they could listen in for free. The players performed twice each day, afternoon and evening, for a couple of hours, but not on Sundays.

It was so pleasant listening to the same old tried and true favorites. Works by Harold, Purcell, G. and S, Offenbach, Strauss and so on. Music which we never seem to tire of. Sometimes a patron might shout out a title for the group to play, and invariably that little band could satisfy each request. On their way to the theater the members of the group would pass by my spot on the promenade and we would exchange greetings.

I boarded at the same guest house as the band, and dinner was quite an experience. Larry Steen was the Leader and Flautist of the group. The only other musician I remember by name was the violinist, Harry, who lived in Birmingham and he would go home for weekends. There were eight other players and every weekday we would have our evening meal together, seated around the huge dining room table at our guest house.

The food served was quite good and sufficient to satisfy everyone's needs. What made dinner-time memorable was that following our usually simple dessert, we would perform a piece from the band's repertoire. Of course, without any instruments.

I had confessed to the leader that I had once played the trumpet, so I was usually assigned that instrument to "play." Harry mouthed the violin while Larry would lead us and mouth the flute. Different parts would be mouthed by the other players. The most amusing aspect of each piece was the way Harry and Larry would vie for the role of conductor. Larry, who arranged most of the music was usually elected the leader of the dining-room orchestra. Harry would pretend to be angry and threaten not to play. We would have a good laugh at these pretend arguments and eventually get down to the business of playing our evening piece. *La Gaza Ladra* was a favorite (the overture, the thieving magpie) as was also Zampa and William Tell. Plenty of noise and lots of fun as we all tried our best to out-do everyone else with our near authentic sounds.

Periodically, Larry would rap on the table and accuse someone of dropping a note or playing in the wrong key. The fake arguments were hilarious as usually Harry was the butt of Larry's objections. It was all in good humor and often the landlady and other guests would gather around to join us in the fun, and add their mouth-music to the general bedlam.

My God, I wonder if other people had as much fun as we did, and what an aid to our digestion of that simple fare. Strangely enough I acquired quite a lot of knowledge about music during that most enjoyable summer.

It would be unfair not to mention Theo Lambert and his band of Harlequin actors who also presented

Aberystwyth 1947 (the author)

entertainment to the visitors, using the same theater pavilion as the orchestra when it had finished it's performance.

Today, I might pay a hundred dollars or more for a theater or concert ticket and find the entertainment not as exciting as what Aberystwyth offered, in 1947.

Lady Mostyn
(Of Mostyn Hall, North Wales, 1947)

The beautiful grounds of Mostyn Hall was open to the public for the annual garden fete. During this special event there were several competitions as well as a wonderful flower show. Rosettes and awards were given for the best in each category. Dogs were also an attraction and they were paraded about and judges would choose the winners.

Not only were dogs in the competition, in a paddock, a small flock of pure, white, fluffy sheep were quietly huddled together. They were looking about anxiously, awaiting their turn, before the judges. Normally sheep don't bathe and have their hair done, this lot looked for all the world like a group of woolly virgins, prepared for their nuptials.

Summers in North Wales are such a joy. The climate is like the people, mild mannered and easy going. Community fairs and idyllic country scenes, as was the case of this fete, spring up like daffodils, across this land of rolling hills. Farming was one of the main industries and traditionally, sheep were the mainstay of many rural ventures.

I happened to be the local photographer in Rhyl, in the adjacent county of Flint. Just a year ago, at the age of twenty, I was at Mostyn Hall and had met the young, Lady Mostyn. *(see the footnote at the end of the story).

I watched her riding a magnificent, chestnut horse. I was there for several hours and that lovely lady never once, for whatever reason, got off that beautiful animal. I wanted to take a photo of Lady Mostyn to be published in the following week's issue of "The Rhyl Journal." The journal paid me a small fee for suitable photos.

Had I been smarter I should have probably called the Hall, in advance to book an appointment to come and take her photo. Alas, I was not comfortable with the protocol and took a chance. Watching that lady, so confident and beautifully dressed, smiling and leaning from her lofty perch, to shake hands with some lucky person.

I could see she was tall and slender, and the thick curls which escaped from under her riding helmet were chestnut colored, adjunct to the handsome gelding she was riding. The Jodhpur's and Harris, Tweed, riding, jacket she was wearing showed her lithe figure, to the best advantage. In my eyes she was like a movie star and yes, my heart began to flutter.

I had drawn some interest when I arrived at the hall, on my new motorcycle, a Velocette 350 Hi Cam, which I rode with pride. I parked beside the jalopies and bicycles and my bright, shiny, motor bike stood out like a beacon. I removed my war-surplus, sheepskin riding jacket and left it secured to the seat of the bike. We didn't wear helmets in those days but I would wear a toque to stop my long hair from flying about. I carried my Leica Camera around my neck, hanging from a leather strap and looked around for possible customers.

If I thought business was possible, I would approach the party, introduce myself and offer my services. Not a lot of people owned cameras in those days, so I could always earn my bread and butter. I took pictures of dogs, sheep, horses and flowers, but could not seem to catch the eye of my main quarry, Lady Mostyn.

Every now and then over a megaphone, a voice would call the attention of the crowd to some event about to take place, like the opening of the refreshment tent, out there on the lawn. This was the highlight of the day. Sandwiches and several barrels of the best beer had been located in the Marquee and the rush was on for lunch. There were quite a number of people standing about in pairs or in small groups, enjoying their food and pints of draught beer. A different crowd frequented an adjoining field participating in friendly horse-races. Their fun seemed to be more of the physical kind.

Then, situated by a small stage, there was a different type of contest. His Lordship, wearing Harris Tweeds and Plus Fours, announced the prize of a guinea for the winner of the Knobby Knees Contest. All men were invited take part in this contest and several did. The men would line up across the stage and roll their trousers above their knees, while the ladies would walk to and fro examining the men's knees. Quite a lot of laughter accompanied the examination, there was prodding and pinching and a lot of giggling, until the winner was announced. The guinea prize was presented to the old, estate, gamekeeper who owned the biggest pair of knees I had ever seen. I took a picture for posterity but it was never used. The prettiest child contest took a serious turn, when the best friends fell out when the winner was chosen.

The two finalists came to blows when the wrong child won the contest. The mothers had to be pulled apart by the stewards and the matter was settled by measuring cheers from the crowd. Lord Mostyn announced a draw and the prize was divided. Later, I looked at the babies to see what the fuss was all about and all I could see were two fat, hairless, balls, of smelly blubber. I wondered why the mothers made such a fuss. Being a grandfather many times over I have since changed my mind about babies.

There was a "judges' tent" where the public were not allowed to enter, reserved for the people in charge of the show. Being a member of the press, I was allowed entry and was offered refreshments. Here there was a nice bar set up with all sorts of spirits and wines, for the more discerning taste.

Several of that elite group wanted a picture of themselves. I took the pictures after I made it clear that there would be a charge up front, with this explanation they appeared to lose interest. It was nearing time for me to leave. I made my way to the parking lot where my heart gave another flutter, as there looking down at my shiny, motor bike was that special lady.

As I approached her, I called out, "Hello, can I take your picture?"

She looked down from that magnificent horse, I thought how well they were matched.

"Alright," she smiled at me and I asked her to move into the light.

After a few minutes when I thought the picture would be just right, I took the shot.

"Thank you," I called out to her, "That picture should be perfect."

With a smile and a wave of her crop she was about to ride away. I remembered my last words, "What about the cost of the photos?"

In such a cheerful manner she replied, "Oh, you don't have to pay," she smiled over her shoulder and rode out of sight.

I never saw her again, and the editor didn't use the pictures and threw them away.

*P.S. What a strange coincidence. This story had deleted itself from my computer and googling "Lady Mostyn" today, (March 25 2017), to research more details, the heading read that "Lady Sheila Mostyn, of Mostyn, North Wales, the last of the family line, has just passed away at the age of eighty nine years."

The author of this story is now in his 90s and the news gave me a strange feeling.

Dreams Of Long Ago - 1949

On the outskirts of that delightful seaside resort, Colwyn Bay, North Wales, there was a double row of nice homes across the low hill south of the sea. We had been meaning to canvass that area to obtain more customers for our photographic products.

In 1949, the most popular camera was the Brownie Box camera. Most homes had at least one and the cost was just a few shillings. Majority of families had photo albums containing small black and white photos. The concept of color photos was some sort of an abstract notion. The odd Hollywood movie had been produced in color, a wonderful example being "Gone with the Wind," however, black and white photography was the norm.

My brother Victor had developed an amazing skill at coloring photographs in "Oils." Our current method of earning a living was by canvassing door to door, with samples of our work. We'd ask the householder if they would like to purchase a special snap copied, colored, framed and enlarged, like the sample which we produced. The price was quite modest and it was by our method of low-cost production that our profit margin was very healthy.

Victor had built a copier out of a few pieces of lumber, two lightbulbs and the front of an old bellows portrait camera. It could not only make a card negative, but with minimum effort and skill serve the purpose of an enlarger. Most negatives were made from film, the processing of which was tedious.

Of course, card negatives were simpler, cleaner and quicker but lacked a little in detail. We would load the snap to be copied in the front rack of the machine, then expose the loaded card, which was enlarged to some extent. Next, we developed the card and after a quick rinse and wipe, repeated the process with the negative in the front rack. Then we adjusted the device to produce a black and white photo approximately eight inches by ten in size. This would be thoroughly washed and dried. Then Victor would perform his magic with his tubes of oil-paint and cotton balls. The end result would be an excellent color portrait.

We tried to standardize the frames so that mounts, glass and backs could quickly fit together, with minimum effort. From old picture frames, household glass etc. we'd obtain the pieces of glass and have them cut to size, for a few pennies at our local hardware store. The mounts or mattes we would cut from white sheets of cardboard. The frame-backs we'd cut with a sharp blade and steel ruler from cardboard boxes we'd collect from local shops. Victor would make variegated lines on the matt and sign the picture "Victor Charles Studio." The entire process would be completed using adhesive paper strips known as "Passe Partout." The finished article would cost the customer two pounds seven shillings and a sixpence, of which most was profit.

The customer r-action to the finished portrait was invariably positive. Victor had learned his special skill from a master. Along with his manipulation of his oils he could deftly improve the subject appearance without in any way changing the basic structure. I admired his artistic skills and found the job of canvassing and door to door selling to be an enjoyable chore, whereby some folks disliked door to door selling immensely.

This particular early fall day in north Wales, I was canvassing Colwyn Bay and knocked at the door of this pleasant two-storey house, complete with its lovely tended garden. Number twelve, Sea View Gardens, an older lady answered the door in response to my knock. Mrs. Price, she called herself. In reply to my standard approach she said, "Well, you better come in."

I entered Mrs. Price's beautiful home. There were knickknacks in shining brass, fine porcelain, highly waxed, Victorian style furniture and the entire ambiance slightly persuaded by a delightful combination of the smell of roses and wax polish.

Mrs. Price was interested in having a picture of her late husband copied and had picked out a place on the salon wall for the picture to rest. While she was rummaging through the drawers of a small antique desk to find her husband's picture, she explained that Mr. Price, a captain in the merchant navy, had been killed in action in 1944. She found the snap of a middle-aged grey-bearded sailor, in the tropical uniform of a navy commander. She said how she wished he could have been wearing his captain's insignia when the snap was taken.

I took charge of the picture, noted color details and received a cash deposit, promising to return with the finished portrait in a week's time. I recounted the story to Victor. With a few strokes to the finished work, he added a fourth gold stripe to Captain Prices shoulder epaulettes.

I delivered the finished work to Mrs. Price as promised and as before was invited into the spotless and beautiful home.

"Oh my God, the picture, I can't believe it, you've got the blue of his eyes exactly right," Mrs. Price cried in an excited voice. "And look you've added his Captain's stripes."

She came over to where I stood and I was lost for a moment or two in an enormous hug.

"Thank you," she added her voice choking with emotion as the record playing on her old Victrola, continued to play.

It was scratchy and brittle, the most beautiful strains of an old Italian song. While this brief transaction took place, my thoughts were torn by conflicting emotions; one being the warm satisfaction of having a very satisfied customer. And the other, the sounds of an unusually beautiful and moving melody. Which was sung by an obviously extraordinary and accomplished tenor voice. I remained standing while the lovely music came to an end.

Mrs. Price paid her account and asked me, "Did you enjoy the record?"

"Oh yes!" I replied "It was absolutely beautiful."

"I've got every record he's ever made," she said as she pointed to her collection of hundreds of records, "I'd like you to have one as a present, in appreciation for this lovely picture."

My protests were brushed aside and finally I chose the old "Victor" slate copy, which had been playing when I arrived (it's still my favorite song). Caruso singing, "Dreams Of Long Ago."

A Bus Ride

This was one of those funny sort of days. I was on a bus in North Wales visiting my mother who lived in Ffynyngroew, have you even been there? It's a pretty little Welsh village, about half way between Aberavon and Lanfairfechan. She resided on the right side of the road, Number Ten, The Cottages, you can't miss it. I was brought up there. A lot of funny things happened to me as I was growing up. That is where I met Myvanwy, and you know what she's like.

Well anyway, I was on that crowded bus sitting beside this great, big, English lady and her daughter; I would say she was about forty or so. To tell you the truth, she took up more than her share of the seat, but that didn't matter to me at all. There was no heat on in the bus, it was winter and bitter cold. I was one of the lucky ones. Sitting there beside that big fat English lady who kept me warm, especially on my left side. As an extra bonus she was quite soft and comfy and smelled like roses.

The actual circumstances meant that only one of my cheeks was on the seat and I teetered a lot. Maneuvering around corners was very precarious, isn't it? The daughter was a pretty girl about my own age. To try to get to know her a little better I would lean over and include her in our conversation. A lot of people tell me they enjoy my sense of humor, however, some folks (mostly English) think the Welsh are a dour lot and not funny at all. Once you learn the language you find out what you've been missing, don't you? Well, we do dig for coal, and we tend sheep and sing a lot, but it comes as a surprise when you discover that we are very funny.

Well, as I was saying, we were about half way there when I was telling a funny story to Ethel, the fat lady's daughter. I suppose her mother thought I was becoming a bit too cheeky, she gave a quick shake of her hips. I went flying and it was only by grabbing onto the big fat lady that I was able to prevent an injury to myself.

That was when the trouble started... Well, I had unintentionally grabbed on to one of the Breasts of the English lady. Being an athletic young fellow I was able to re-establish myself onto my part of the seat. There I was, holding on to that haven when she began to call out to the driver that she was being molested. Being a gentleman, I was immediately ready to defend the lady's honor.

When to my horror, I was the one being accused. I let go of the breast and apologized. It was then that I discovered that it was the English who seemed to be lacking in a sense of humor. She insisted that the police being called at the next stop and that I be charged with the affront. What a disgrace, and me still a virgin. I begged the lady not to press charges and soon she realized that it had been a nasty accident, after all. She did insist that as a settlement she wanted to hear a funny story.

Fair enough, so I proceeded to tell her the old favorite of the travelling salesman, the farmer's daughter and the monkey, didn't I? Well the joke is a regular at all the Welsh Music Halls and is a bit of a shaggy dog story. I should have told her I was a Welsh Comedian as she didn't understand one word of it. At the end of the story the whole bus-load broke out in laughter.

She was the only one with a straight face in the bus. She complained that she had been cheated, but then she asked me to tell her the story in English so she could have a laugh too. She didn't like it when I told her that the story was not funny in English but I would tell her when she learned to speak Welsh. I then told her I knew a yarn about a gambling Tom-cat who used to put all he had in the Kitty and another about the two rabbits hopping down the road, one stopped and the other hopped on...

To which she replied, "Okay tell me those."

Canada Or Australia -1952

For months I had been dithering. Should I or shouldn't I emigrate? There was the question of destination, if it had been a matter of just going, with no formalities, I would have probably gone to the United States. The influence of books and movies by that time was deep-rooted in my psyche. Several fabulous Commonwealth countries also lured young people into adventure, but at the end of the day, the choice for me was either Canada or Australia. We had heard that proofs of work experience were not as necessary as a strong work ethic.

Many energetic and enterprising men and women left their native land to seek new opportunities far from their tired old country, which was riddled with class and choked by the old school tie. They wanted to escape the self-satisfied and the smug, hanging on for dear life to the way things were.

These adventurers, most of whom had little cash, worked hard and though there were those in these adopted countries who were derisive and scorning, by and large the residents of the new countries were very welcoming.

My friend Harry was travelling to Sydney, Australia, on board the SS Georgic out of Liverpool, England, on November 19th 1952. I was in the line-up of fifty or so last-minute travelers, who were waiting to pay for their tickets, before climbing the long gangway to that enormous ocean liner. I noticed Harry on the forward main deck looking over the rails in my direction. He was waving and shouting instructions to me but his message was totally incomprehensible.

All of a sudden it was my turn at the ticket kiosk, the cashier was a very young blonde girl who smiled at me and said the last minute fare was £105. At that moment I had in my possession the sum total of my worth, £100 and a few shillings in coin. There were a few people left in the line, it was nearly noon, the departure time of the ship. I stood to one side while those last travelers bought their ticket and were on their way. I looked up at the huge ship and there was my friend Harry, his hat in his hand, still waving encouragement.

This was a crisis point of my life. I returned to the cashier and told her I only had £100 and couldn't go. The girl, a total stranger to me, seemed disappointed for me and offered £5 which she said I could pay back when I got a job. Even though this kind offer was tempting and I did express my thanks, I decided against going. The thought of going 10,000 miles and arriving in a strange country with no job or money was no longer interesting.

I went to the front of the boat and shouting up to Harry. I tried to tell him my problem. At the point where he understood that I was short of cash, he produced bank notes and waving them in my direction I could just catch enough of his words to understand that he was offering them to me. The ship's horn at that moment gave a tremendous blast and the gangway was removed and the ship was slowly maneuvered away from the dock to begin its voyage. A gust of wind seemed to catch Harry, and the notes he was waving in my direction were blown out of his hand and landed out in the Mersey River.

I stood there on the quay-side for a long time. Harry and I periodically exchanging waves. Over the years I've sometimes thought about those decisive moments and how things might have been. I believe the trip to Sydney took four weeks in those days and balmy weather would greet them. When the SS Georgic was out in the river's center and I could no longer see people on the deck, I went one more time to the kiosk and learned that a ship was leaving for Canada the following day: Manchester to Halifax via the Manchester Ship Canal. The ship was the Manchester Spinner, an 8,000-ton passenger/cargo ship. The fare was £65.

I took a bus to Manchester and then a cab to the boat dock. I became the sixth passenger on the ship's manifest and settled in to my own private cabin. Most of the night I spent on the ship's deck while we passed under our own steam through the narrow canal system. Slowly the big ocean ship, with only a few feet clearance on each side, made its way along. I watched, thrilled, as we sailed through the suburbs of Manchester and several other small towns and villages. By breakfast, we quietly entered the Mersey and made our way to the Atlantic Ocean.

We were ten days onboard. Most of the time, it was stormy weather and bitterly cold. Whereas the Georgic was heading south into pleasant weather, we on the Manchester Spinner were heading for a climate that would shock first time visitors.

The trip, though rough, was very pleasant. The passenger accommodation was superb, designed to carry a maximum of twelve paying guests, so as we were only six, there was more than enough space. We were served first-class meals.

The bar was available 24 hours a day, though most of us were non-drinkers. Mr. and Mrs. McAlister occupied the next cabin to mine and we became good shipboard friends. We passed the days quietly playing bridge or cribbage and watching the big grey seas slide past the hull. Once in a while a bigger wave would break over our bow and send torrents of water over the ship's deck. Had the trip been longer, I would probably become bored with the repetitious, daily, routine and seascape.

Ten days from Manchester to Halifax and not another ship in view the entire time. Suddenly we approached our first port of call, an overnight stop in St. Johns. We weren't allowed to disembark, but as the weather was cold and wet, no one wanted to leave anyway. The next morning we were once more at sea, it was now December the 2nd. Soon we were docking at Halifax, Nova Scotia.

It was a busy place. Other ships were releasing their human cargo. While I waited for landing formalities I was allowed to go for a walk through the center of the city. I went to the end of Main Street. The public toilets were available in a wrought iron building. In the UK, public toilets are available as a matter of course. The facilities were plain but clean. Public sensibility was protected as these facilities were known as Comfort Stations. I seem to remember that in France similar facilities are quite common and are known as Pissoirs.

I bought a ticket to Montreal on the CNR train. I hadn't spent anything yet, and suddenly more than half my money was gone on the fare. Once onboard the crowded train, everyone settled down for the long train ride to Montreal. The co-travelers in my coach were a group of young men aged about 25 to 30, and it wasn't long before we were chatting and having fun. Then out came the cards and a poker game started. Several times I was asked to play. Finally, I told them I only had a few dollars left and what my plans were.

They seemed to understand my predicament and continued to include me in their conversation. In the morning the train steward went through the aisles calling for "First Breakfast." The dining car was now open. My fellow passengers took off for breakfast, but I declined. The group insisted that I join them as their guest. I gratefully enjoyed a good breakfast and thanked them. I thought what kind and generous people Canadians are.

At Montreal, we said goodbye and I was left to my own devices for a few hours until my friend Keith came home from work. My clothes were suitable for the mild English climate and though they were smart enough, they did little to protect me from the bitter cold. I stayed inside as much as possible until around 5pm when I was able to contact him by phone. We chatted awhile and when I told him I had no place to stay he said "Come to my place, my landlady is looking for another boarder." I took a streetcar to Verdun and met his landlady, who rented me a room with board for twenty dollars a week.

Now my main problem was a job. I was lucky, even though jobs did not exactly go begging, I was up and about every day knocking at doors. By the end of the week I managed to find something suitable to start me on my new life.

The CNR hired me as a research clerk for $40 a week. My take-home pay was $36.50. The tram fare was 25 cents daily. Here I was, settled and working in a good job, able to pay my way and money left over for all sorts of exciting activities. Things were certainly looking up, and it crossed my mind that my friend Harry had not even reached Australia yet and here was I already on my way to fame and fortune.

Brian's Boat

One of my friends in Southern England, dreamt of sailing the world. He saw himself at the helm of a sleek yacht with the warm, salt, spray of some enchanted sea, caressing his suntanned chest. He saw himself with his keen, brown, eyes guiding his eager ship to places with exotic charm. The seas of the world's warm places, beckoned this modern-day adventurer. He wished to travel to those story-book lands, where history records the brave exploits of villains and heroes, in an age long past.

What marvelous ideas float through the dreams of the lucky ones who entertain romantic notions, anticipation and do the planning, which often acts as their own reward. Though more often the romantic dreams seldom become reality, man can be sustained without the climax of accomplishment. How much better when some chance spark ignites thought to action and brings a dream to reality.

Brian, my British friend, skimmed across the periphery of a working world, engaged in jobs which rarely exploited his talents, nor earned him a decent living. He gathered experiences in mundane trades which brought him no nearer to his dreams but merely sustained him in his hum-drum life. Peaks of joy were experienced as each new job was secured, or a new love discovered or both. However, always unwittingly and unknowingly the work of fate adjusted his life, to bring him closer to his goal.

Chance caused Brian to apply for a position as Stage Manager in a Southerly-located, English theatre. This general-factotum job, primarily included the creating and building of stage-sets, against which the theater's plays could be presented. He landed the job and in learning his new trade, Brian grew to love the feel and smell of freshly-worked wood. In his eagerness to express his creative senses, he quickly mastered the basic carpentry skills that were required.

Brian built bigger and better sets and with each new experience he improved his chances to reach his goal. These were the early sixties, jobs were plentiful but wages in the theatre were low, to say the least. There were many fringe benefits but specifically for Brian, the off-cut, scrap, pieces of wood and the old discarded sets were there for the taking. Squirreling away the bits and pieces and along with his successful scrounging, he was at last ready for his Opus Magnum.

Night after night he laboured with pencil and paper, creating hundreds of sketches of boats of different sizes and models. At last his efforts found one drawing which caught his fancy. He focused his interest as he drew a sleek yacht of 26 feet in length with a beam of 8 feet and Bermuda Rigged, which seemed to suit his needs. From his drawing he developed his blue-prints. He rented space by an old, deserted, wharf-side warehouse. At the age of thirty four he laid the keel and was on his way to fulfill his dreams.

Slowly the bits and pieces were augmented by purchases made from the money he earned. His daily walks would produce results as they led him past dock-sides and harbor-fronts where he would glean advice and information from those more skilled than he. Wood, canvas screws, nails and glue were gradually molded, through sheer patience, into a distinctive shape. Three years of struggle and trial and error was finally paying off. The language of sail was mostly learned in the dockside pubs of old Bristol Town. To learn the sailor's jargon was an apprenticeship in another tongue, fore and aft, port and starboard, halyard, mainstay and jenny, abeam, abaft, luft and reef, and so on. He was entering the exciting world of sail.

Each day he brought new dimensions of thought and skill to the project. Three years of scrounging, testing, trying, learning and orchestrating his energies to reach the first step. He stood back to take it all in and enjoy the remarkable thrill of achievement--the craft complete except for rigging and cosmetics. What a beautiful sight it was. Brian gazed at his work, a product of his own excitement. He looked at his worn and calloused hands, clenched his fists, raised them shoulder high and shouted and laughed with joy.

In his entire life Brian had never accomplished anything remotely compared to the crafting of his beautiful, new boat. Now funds were exhausted and he was requiring a few more hundred pounds to prepare the boat to be sea worthy. Two strokes of good fortune had just happened. The first was in the form of a sponsorship from Mr. Wexford, the owner of a large lumber mill nearby. The second stroke of luck was seeing an advertisement in the Bristol Times calling for participants in a yacht race.

Mr. Wexford had been in the habit of taking a daily walk along the docks in the vicinity. Unknown, to Brian he had been observing him working and had been fascinated at his dogged determination. Over time he had witnessed changes to the level of Brian's skill with only the bare minimum of tools and help and these traits had earned Wexford's respect. Wexford now sensed he could help Brian and at the same time help himself. Mr. Wexford offered to provide the funds for the rigging and cosmetics and other needs, in order to be ready for the big race. The condition being that Wexford's name be prominently displayed on the boat's hull. The agreement meant Brian's money worries were over. The following day an order was placed at the Sail-Maker's.

The advertisement appearing in the "Bristol Times" indicated that a sailboat race was to take place from the Isle of Wight to the Channel Islands and return, under sail. All home-built boats 16 to 30 feet were eligible to enter. A prize of 5,000 pounds was being offered to the winner. The race would take place that same year and commence at noon on August the first, just four months away. Application forms could be obtained from the Times office, where along with a competitors number a list of race rules would be provided.

The next day Brian was the first customer and his number was "223." The race would start at noon sharp. No motors were allowed. Basic emergency equipment was mandatory including a radio. Maximum crew, per boat being two. Each boat would leave Cowes harbor on the Isle of Wight and sail around Jersey where race-officials would register the boat passing the check-point, and confirming the transaction by firing a red flare. Landing anywhere en-route, for any reason, would result in disqualification.

The trip around the Channel Islands was very straight-forward, merely tacking out of Cowes and heading south-west for a pleasant sail. It's always warm that time of year, the water of the Gulf Stream separates in the Atlantic and gently divides itself to flow around Britain. As a result, the temperature of the water in the Channel is quite moderate. The distance from the Isle of Wight to the Channel Islands is about a hundred miles or so. Brian estimated the pace of the race at thirty miles a day which would mean about nine days at sea. So to be on the safe side, he would victual for eighteen days.

The most Brian had ever sailed was on the reservoir near Bristol, a lake about two miles across. The other experience was the narrows of the River Severn. He'd be out of sight of land for several days so whoever crewed for him would have to possess navigational skills.

Now as the days were stretching and becoming longer and warmer, painting the boat was a pleasant chore. Brian tried a new twist, using a synthetic glue he covered the entire boat's exterior with mercerized cotton and then applied several coats of marine paint. Proudly he painted his Race numbers on each side of the hull in two foot high figures, number "223." Followed in small print were the words, "or bust." The next stage of his preparations was to obtain food and water for the trip, and of course, bring a case of 24 strong beer, just in case of an emergency.

The days began to move along, and at last the rigging and sails arrived from the Sail-maker. It took two weeks to fit, adjust and fine-tune them to the boat. Mr. Wexford arranged to ship the boat across England and settle it in the peaceful waters, off the South Coast where the Solent enters the Channel. Meanwhile, back in Bristol with only nine days before the race, Brian realizing a solo trip was out of the question, visited the dockside cafes and pubs looking for someone to crew with him. Earlier that year he had met Harry Towne, a tall, skinny, forty-year-old with a crop of mousey hair, a habitue of the "Coat Of Arms" pub.

Brian entered the pub and asked for his usual pint, adding, "I'm looking for a crew for the big race, do you know of anyone?"

"Not really," the Barman replied, "Around here lots of men would love to go but at this time of the year they would all have commitments."

Brian sipped on his beer. At this point Harry sidled up and tapped Brian on the shoulder, "I'll go," he said.

The interview that followed was lively, with the topping up of several pints of strong beer and finally a deal was struck. Harry convinced Brian by claiming to have sailed to Cherbourg several times and the few extra miles around Jersey was to him, "No big deal."

So at last all the loose ends had been connected, they would join the "223" on the last day of July, which was in just a few days.

The port of Cowes was crowded with boats of all sizes and description. Hundreds more were packed in the reaches of the Solent Inlet. It was a lovely summer's day as 500 boats made their final moves, while waiting for the canon report which would officially start the race. Brian and Harry were eager and ready, and still hoping the work ahead and the open air would clear their hangover, from the pub-crawl of the previous night.

Their plan was simple, upon leaving port, they would navigate the east reach of the Isle of Wight and once in the English Channel, set sail and steer toward the Cherbourg Peninsula and to Pas Cap de la Hague, on their Port Beam. Then they planned to proceed south staying in sight of France, on the port side until they came in sight of Jersey to the starboard. At that point they would steer west, close in to the Jersey shore, past St. Hilier, the Capitol. Then it was time to stand by for the acknowledgement signal. The next step was to proceed on a northwest course past Guernsey, then head directly North for Cowes and ready to be awarded the prize of five thousand pounds.

At noon the boom of the cannon echoed across Cowes Harbor and more than four hundred boats raised sail, the day was perfect. There was a light, northeast breeze which made it necessary to tack often to make any headway at all. Two hours passed before they were out from Hyde and just three miles from where they started. Soon Brian and his crew were able to function as a team and tacking became less of a chore. By six p.m., they were at the point of passing the eastern extremity of the Island. This was a place called Bembridge and lay ahead was the full width of the English Channel.

Now the sightseers, in their boats had almost all bid their friends "God Speed," and "Good Luck" and returned to the comfort of their secluded moorings. The racers had begun to spread out across the waves. Several mini-collisions had lessened the number of contestants, thankfully, no-one had been hurt. With the Isle of Wight creeping slowly by on their starboard beam.

Harry called out, "Steer 195 degrees," adding "If the wind keeps up we'll see Cherbourg the day after tomorrow."

The north-east breeze had freshened and was beginning to speed them on their way. The knot-reader was indicating a nice 2.4 knots. It was Brian's watch and the plan was that each would spend four hours on watch and four off, so they could rest and stay alert. At around nine p.m. when the sun was low on the horizon, the wind had subsided and the boat's progress dropped to just above one knot. This was the situation as Brian gave the tiller to Harry and made himself comfortable in the cabin, sleep eventually came. At midnight Harry's call meant a change of shift. These circumstances continued for two more days when Brian checked with Harry to see if they were still on course.

"Sure," he said "You have to trust me."

The following morning just as the sun was rising, Harry called out "Looks like land dead ahead."

Slowly the boat sloshed its way toward what appeared to be a major port, in a wide expanse of shore.

Passing a French fishing boat Brian called out "Where are we?"

"Caen" was the cheerful reply.

Brian acknowledged the fishermen and turned to Harry who had disappeared into the cabin.

"Where the hell are you Harry? "This is Caen, I thought you said you could navigate!"

Sheepishly, Harry acknowledged his error, "Sorry, I forgot the Channel tide."

Brian now realized Harry had exaggerated his ability to navigate but as they were half way out he realized it was too late to do anything about it. The revised course was set to get their craft back on track.

By noon on the next day with a following breeze, Cap de la Hague became visible off the port beam. They started a southern course passing the Cherbourg Peninsula. The boat began to pick up speed.

They sailed past the Isle of St. Anne on their right and Harry shouted "twenty miles and we'll be passing Jersey."

The wind was strengthening and at first light, there in the distance was the half-way mark, Jersey, and on its south coast was St. Hellier, the capitol. This passing was confirmed by officials on the shore. There were no other boats in sight. When Brian again took his turn sleeping, he noticed a rolling sound, in the scuppers and discovered there were several empty beer cans. Checking his case of beer he found that they had all been consumed.

In a rage he leapt to the deck and confronted Harry, who said, "I'm sorry but I couldn't help myself."

Reluctantly Brian returned to rest.

The sky had turned leaden and the waves rose higher. An angry Brian took his turn at the helm and reefed his sail for a blow. As darkness fell, a full gale struck the little craft which rode the seas like a wild thing. With the wind whistling in the taut steel lines, it made a horrible screaming noise. The boat was reefed for a storm with all gear stowed, there was no recourse except to ride it out. At the end of his watch, an exhausted Brian tied down the helm and went inside to get his relief.

Entering the cabin he was confronted by a horrible sight. There on the deck lay Harry, terrified of rough weather, clutching his knees in a fetal position and blubbering in fear like a child. With curses and blows Brian tried to restore some sort of order, however, nothing helped. He returned to the cockpit, tied himself down with a spare line and prepared to hold on till the storm had passed.

Hours later when the storm had done its worst the sturdy boat was still making headway though half full of the cold, dark, sea. Harry came forward and apologized for his behavior.

Still filled with rage and disappointment Brian replied "Never mind Harry, we'll be passing Guernsey any time now, and you'll be getting off."

Harry, in silence, slunk back to the cabin and began to bail.

About an hour passed and off to the starboard, the Isle of Guernsey appeared. Sailing close to shore Brian called Harry to the cockpit and following a short scuffle Harry was thrown over the side followed by a lifebelt, to make his way to shore. The weather continued to improve and Brian set his course northward. Once again, securing himself in the cockpit with a life-line, he managed to get some shut eye.

So the trip home passed, a long tedious four days and there ahead was the most beautiful sight, the coast of Southern England. He steered to the east, toward the reaches of the Solent and the peace and safety of Cowes. He was the 313th contestant to make it back to port. The experience of his success was the first of many to come.

Eventually a newspaper reporter interviewed my friend and asked him how things went. His modest reply was, "Had a lovely trip, thank you."

The reporter then asked Brian "What do you think of the Daily Express Single hand sail around Britain next year?"

Brian sat up straight in his chair, bearing a big grin, "Is that so?," he asked. "Tell me more about it."

Post script:

Harry built a 40 foot sloop with an eleven-foot beam for that race around Britain. He built it in the upper floor of a riverside barn. When the hull was completed a contact in the RAF helped to transfer the boat to the river by helicopter, where they were able to attach the concrete Keel. First things first they had to remove the roof from the barn to get the boat out. It went through my mind how the sailing community had so many devious ways to cut corners to achieve their goals. Here was my friend Brian, moneyless as usual, basking in the rays of his success. When we saw him in Bristol that summer he hardly had time to chat.

Pete Crone

When I met Pete Crone, he was a semi-retired gentleman operating a general store with his wife. The store was known as "The Log Cabin" it was located on Innisfil Beach Road, a few miles south of Barrie, Ontario. We had built a cottage next door to his place and met over the garden fence. Then we spent some interesting times helping each other do chores on our properties. I got to know Pete and introduced myself and was addressing him as Mr. Crone.

He said "Don't call me Mister, I won't know who you are talking to, call me Pete, everyone does." (*Refer to the footnote at the end of the story). So from the start we were on quite personal terms. Pete was in his seventies, small, maybe five foot three, slight and with a wiry build. Thinning white hair, one of those people you take to right away. He seemed to be a happy man with a smile close to his lips and eyes.

Pete's wife was about his age, a roundish lady with cheerful red cheeks and always pleasant to my wife and five small children. It is always fortunate to have neighbors like that, they were polite, kind and friendly yet never pried into our personal business. After a few years we sold our place and lost touch. Later, we learned that Pete had passed away and his wife had moved into a condo in the town.

Pete Crone, it was not difficult to admire a man like that. He was always ready with a hello and a cheerful word, though sometimes his asthmatic wheeze made it difficult to understand him. Eventually, he did stop at our house for a cup of tea, and for the first time he didn't seem in a rush to leave. He never talked about himself, and I wondered where his North Country accent and way of speech came from. This was the time I was able to satisfy my inquisitive nature. I had been quite open about my background, and I had told him how I came to Canada, from Wales and joined the airline in 1953. He told me a very short story about his coming to Canada and his life back then.

"Yes Trev," he said, as I poured him another cup of tea. "I always thought of myself as a lucky stiff. I was a young lad in Yorkshire, you know how things were for the poor when England proudly ruled most of the world. While thousands and thousands of starving children lived on the streets. I was a small skinny lad and eventually put in the poorhouse, I was thirteen when that happened. I remember how we used to eat watery porridge, twice a day, but you know, it was a darn sight better than nothing. I wasn't there for more than a few months, when on my fourteenth birthday I was taken by the Beadle where I was told that I had been chosen to go to Canada."

"My benefactor was a rancher in Medicine Hat, Alberta. Soon I was packed and I was on my way, in the clothes I was wearing, and I brought an extra pair of pants, underwear and boots in a small kit-bag. These extras were provided by a local church group, and my ticket was purchased by my benefactor."

"I don't remember a lot about that trip half way round the world. Several of us boys were shipped out. The ship smelled like sick and the noise of the engines was awful, but at least it was warm. It was 1912 and soon we were on our way."

"Weren't you scared?" I asked, quite caught up in the tale.

"I don't really recall how I felt. I was scared and excited at the same time. I had been given a little book about Canada which I had read over and over. I was very keen to be going to that beautiful land, which flowed with milk and honey. My dream of the kind family who wanted me and had paid all that money for me to go and live with them, was vivid in my mind."

We were ship-board a long time when unusual noises and crew-members running around made me think that we had at last arrived at our destination. The sailor I asked told me, "Don't be daft, this is Queenstown, (Cork) Ireland."

We were there for a day until every space that a person could fit had been filled and we were once more on our way. I have no idea how long we were there on that awful ship. Day after day and week after week of rolling and swaying and pounding through those terrible seas. We lay exhausted, too sick to eat. The noise of the engines accompanied by the moaning and the retching of the passengers prevented sleep, except for an occasional nap once in a while, it was not pleasant.

Eventually, the sea became fairly smooth and with food being plentiful it didn't seem so bad. After what seemed like a lifetime we landed at Halifax. At last we were there, my new home, but my hopes were suddenly dashed, I was sent to the train station where I was told that Medicine Hat was still thousands of miles away. I was another week on that train when finally we arrived at Medicine Hat. Here I was at last. A small, skinny, confused kid in a weird wild country, peering out of the grimy train window, trying to identify someone from my future home. I departed from the train, there was no-one there to meet me.

After a few minutes a man in a railroad uniform called out, "Hey Kid, are you Pete, going to the Circle K?"

"Yes sir" I replied, and I was directed to a stage coach with two horses attached, where another wild ride began. I was told to get off at River Junction. Finally at that depot, I was informed to walk east a few miles and on the other side of the hill I would find the Circle K. It was like I was going no-where in a strange night-mare. I headed down the path, which seemed to be a trail made by animals. There were thousands of head of cattle spread all over the wild countryside. Suddenly, coming toward me, galloping across that prairie was a man with a second horse in tow. As he came close he yelled "Pete." "Yes, it's me," I replied and I was told to climb aboard. That was the first time I was ever on a horse. A short time later we arrived at the Circle K.

The man who had come to meet me was called Shorty, how well his nickname suited him. He was about my height, but stocky with bandy legs. We headed straight ahead to a long, low, shed which was the bunkhouse. My new friend showed me where I would sleep. Then he took me to the kitchen, where about twenty cowboys were seated at a long table eating roast beef, potatoes and cabbage. I was given a big plate of food and though I was almost dropping with fatigue, I made short work of it.

Eventually, I turned into my bunk and was asleep until awakened by the sound of a bell calling the cowboys to breakfast. Well, the next few days went by like a blur. I stuck close to Shorty who showed me the ropes and so much more. He taught me how to ride and care for that old, club-footed, horse that was given to me.

Charlie, my horse, was dark and patient, one of the boys shouted, "Watch that hoss kid, keep him on a tight rein, as he likes to go in circles, his foot makes him do it." Charlie, the horse was born on the ranch and everyone said that if I get lost, just give him his head and he would bring me home.

Then I was given my first real job by the foreman, I was to go fence-riding. The tools, a bed-roll, a roll of wire and a sack of food were attached to the saddle. Just before leaving, Shorty handed me a Colt revolver to be used against snakes and other dangerous animals I might encounter. I didn't know it at the time that the firing pin had been filed off just in case I might have an accident and shoot myself.

On that ride I learnt that the Circle K Ranch was as big as a small country. That first day I rode to the south border of the ranch and fixed several small breaks in the fence. I slept in my bed-roll with the starred sky above. I listened to the howling of some strange animals and slept with my pistol in my hand. I was on my own for four days, totally alone, my only company being Charlie and now and then a herd of cows. My supply of wire was used up and it was time to head for home. At the crack of dawn I awoke, packed up my kit and giving Charlie his head, made my way back to the ranch house, some fifteen miles away.

Before dark we arrived back at the ranch and it was great to be welcomed by the foreman with a wave and "Hi Pete," just like I was one of the other cowboys. With a new level of confidence I took my place at the table and joined in the conversation. I was given a cigarette and learned to smoke. I turned in that night with the feeling that for the first time in my life I was a real person. I was a man with a job, I was actually working and earning my own way. That night I slept amid the snores and noises of my fellow cowboys and with a smile on my face which wouldn't wear off."

Post script

Years later when thinking about that conversation with that fine man, it went through my mind that some of those great estates in Alberta, might have been owned by corporations in England. Perhaps Pete and the other boys who were sent out to Canada, might have had their tickets purchased by the company for whom they were being conscripted to work. Either way the lives of those orphan boys were changed for the better, in that regard they could be called the benefactors.

The Canoe Trip

I was fifty years of age that year (1977) and at the same time I had worked for the Airline for twenty five years. Surely, the combination of these two critical anniversaries called for some special accomplishment. It was because of these two milestones that I decided to celebrate the occasion. Canoeing seemed to be the way to go, from Reading to Bath, England, via the Kennet and Avon canal. Being a very proud employee of our national airline I decided that I would travel on the almost defunct canal. I would be carrying our company logo proudly on the bow of the little boat. The name "Canada" would be displayed near its stern. I had encouraged my brother, three years my junior, to accompany me on this adventure.

To prepare myself for what I thought might include serious hardship, I joined the "Y" to work out and started my jogging exercises. Within a few months I had improved my physical endurance and shed almost twenty pounds of surplus fat. I realized that the canal system was over a hundred miles long. There was an average of over one lock for every mile of its length so that would involve a lot of rowing.

I studied pamphlets, maps and articles dealing with the Kennet and Avon Canal system. I also spent some time in the United Kingdom Public Records Office, at Kew Gardens, learning more historic details of the waterway. I was surprised that a canal, originally referred to as a "Navigation," could be so interesting.

While I was studying the micro-film at the Public Records Office, I learned that a group of wealthy landowners had arranged an act of parliament. This brought the "Kennet and Avon Canal Co." into existence. The company was given the right to expropriate all the lands required to complete their charter. Engineers planned the building of

A group of boys we met en route.

this huge project, which would connect Reading with Bath and allow travelers to cross England between these cities, in comfort and safety. Besides, it would be cheaper and faster than the alternate mode of travel at that time.

Once opened to the public in the early 1800's, much private and barge traffic was expected. The owners of the canal and their transport services were expressly given the right to proceed to the head of the traffic line, at the locks. With this authority in place, very fast service could be provided to the traveling and freighting public, between these two very important cities.

At Reading, travelers could ride to London via rapid horse and carriage service, or alternatively continue by comfortable passenger barge, in a more leisurely manner, by way of the River Thames. There was so much information dealing with the "Kennet and Avon Canal," including the political questions, legalities, wonderful engineering achievements, labor and social questions and anecdotes. All of that was more than ample information provided by a small library.

Digging a one hundred mile trench using primitive tools and lining the ditch with waterproof clay, is in itself almost a miracle. There was no army of unskilled labor standing by, waiting to be hired. Available manpower had gone to the smoke-filled city factories, stooped and grey-faced, manufacturing beads, widgets, textiles and whatnots, for export all over the world. The Canal Company sent representatives to Ireland and thousands of young Irish were hired as "Navigators," soon to become known as "Navvies." These men required no special skills but were required to be big, strong, in good health and maintain a good work ethic.

The heartiest of the men, paid at three pence per yard of earth removed, could earn more than they had ever earned before. There were no social services available during those years. This homogenous labor force somehow provided for their own. As the locks and lockmasters' houses were completed and staffed, victims of accident or illness were given nursing care, in makeshift hospital rooms. These were provided by the lockmaster's wife, paid for by an early form of mutual benefit scheme, organized and paid for by the workers.

The friendly crew of this cruiser served us tea and cakes

Civil and mechanical engineers did tremendous work. Especially at the step locks at Devizes, the highest point of the canal. This section of the canal was the subject of a recent re-building project. It can be clearly observed that this series of locks and their water supply, were obviously an exceptional engineering achievement. Particularly, when seen from the viewpoint that construction was started in the year 1800. From Devizes to the west the altitude drops to almost sea level, at Bath. From this point to the west the altitude descends more slowly. We have the genius of Isombard Kingdom Brunell to thank for the design and structure of enormous water pumps. These were buried deep in the earth, which provided the water which made the canal system functional.

Today, the canal in places is in a serious state of disrepair and much of it is dry and unusable. However, hundreds of volunteers and other dedicated workers, as well as public subscriptions and very minor government funding, are all helping to turn the tide of decay. Slowly, miles are being added to the usable distance of this valuable recreational property.

My first chore was a rather difficult one, transporting the boat from Toronto to London. One of our corporate perks was an annual discount pass allowing each employee, once each year, to ship via airfreight up to one hundred pounds of goods. Employees were given a 75% discount. The problem with taking advantage of this generous offer was the vol-

Typical scene on the British canal system.

ume/weight ratio. The canoe, at fifteen feet with a 36 inch beam created a large volume, albeit not a significant weight. Also my package was three feet longer than the biggest stowage on the B747, on which I planned to travel, on the first leg of the trip. The problem of the stowage was discussed by colleagues, who had become interested in my project. It was the duty manager who had come up with a solution.

The rear-most cargo compartment was an area about twelve feet in length. The aircraft tail section was secured separate to the cargo, by a powerful network of webbing straps, approximately nine inches apart. Disconnecting one hook and connecting it to the adjacent ring would allow a space for the pointed end of the canoe. I called in a favor and the volume factor in calculating my waybill was cancelled. I paid my bill of fifty dollars and was on my way.

I had booked a Mini in the U.K., complete with a roof rack. I picked up the car from the rental agency after clearing arrival formalities. Then I returned to the airport cargo terminal to pick up my canoe. Here I was presented with another problem, as I encountered Her Majesty's Water Guard, alias, British Customs. There were apparently some restrictions in the importation of this type of boat. Eventually, my pleas were successful and a temporary import license was issued to me. I loaded my boat and was ready for the adventure.

My brother and I met at Reading, as arranged, and launched our loaded boat into the water. It was just a short distance from where the river Kennet met the Thames. I then returned the mini to the Standard Tours rental office.

We noticed that the gunwale of our loaded craft was only a few inches above the river's undulating surface. As we continued upstream we had to navigate through an area of rough water. We were relieved we had brought a small, two horse power, outboard motor amongst our kit. This extra power enabled us to push our way against the fast flowing current.

This particular stretch of the river flowed through the warehouse and industrial section of the city. Some workers were spending a work break exercising their racing pigeons. One of the pigeons had skimmed too close to the water and had become wet and was unable to fly properly. It was in danger of drowning. The owner began to scream at us to rescue the bird. Unfortunately, we couldn't help the bird as we were on the point of capsizing. The bird-fancier, thinking we were cruelly ignoring the bird's plight, changed his calls for help to actual threats of bodily harm. We left that area as fast as we could, without capsizing and were pleased to reach quiet water.

We continued for a while where the water and the grassy banks of the river seemed like a refuge for many birds and small animals. It was the month of May and in following after a mother duck, with twelve, tiny baby ducklings, we inadvertently entered a shallow area. A hidden rock knocked our tiny motor off the transom. It disappeared amongst the grassy waters. So ended our first day.

Retrieving our motor and re-tracing our route to the junction of the Kennet and the Thames, we had noticed a canal boat marina. It was just a short distance from the huge, ugly gas tanks, which marred what should have been a picturesque scene.

We met Graham and his wife Barbara who operated the marina. Graham told us where the dealer was located to repair our motor. He offered us the choice of three of his canal boats to use in the meantime, until our motor was repaired. We secured the canoe to the nearest of the canal boats and settled in for what was to become a two day wait. Shortly after, Graham called us to accompany him to his house for supper. We had a very nice meal and spent the evening with this very charming and generous couple. Later, we all strolled along the path beside the river then spent a pleasant hour at the local pub.

Finally the motor was ready, Graham drove us to the dealership to pick it up. Before noon we were again on our way. We were shown a short-cut to the canal just this side of the first lock. With Graham's guidance we did not have to repeat the first day's stresses. Offers of payment for our accommodations etc. were brushed aside and we parted with promises to return.

We had obtained our license to use the canal, from the British Waterways Board office, near Marylebone, in London. We had declined the rental of a lock key. We felt that the added weight of the big, iron lock-key would off-set its benefits. A small cabin cruiser was entering the lock as we approached and we entered the system with it. Now we were safe in the gentle water of the canal. The maximum speed allowable in the canal was four miles per hour. This speed limit was to reduce erosion of the earthworks, from any speeding boat's wake. It presented no difficulty for us, as our effort at paddling brought us no where near the allowable speed. Adding the occasional use of our motor our maximum speed was not more than the legal allowable.

We had entered into another world. The weather was superb; a clear blue sky, a light breeze and the forecast promising several days of warm weather. As we proceeded along the canal we just enjoyed its peace and tranquility. Ahead of us, we could see, way off in the distance, the lonely cruiser with which we had entered the waterway. Behind us, disappearing slowly but surely, was the skyline of Reading. This was indeed a bucolic paradise. Periodically we passed under charming bridges that were often going nowhere.

Over the years, most of the locks on this system had become communities. The mode of power at the inception of the canal was horse or manpower. Tow paths had been built on each side of the waterway. These rights of way, though now seldom used by horses had become public footpaths. Rambling associations and others, kept these paths in use and thus prevented the landowners from re-asserting their private ownership.

We questioned this matter and were assured that the owners of the land through which the footpaths pass, could enclose the property. If it wasn't used for a year or more. Of the many countries I've traveled to over the years, the United Kingdom is singular in its footpaths, bridle paths and public rights of way. There are thousands of miles of what are sometimes referred to as linear parks. I believe it would be tragic if this park resource would be lost.

During that first day while slowly proceeding along the canal, small children would appear on the towpaths and wave or tease us. We'd stop and chat with kids and others and they were very interested in our craft. The typical canoe in the U.K. is quite different to what we refer to as a canoe. Theirs is similar to our kayak, and by the interest shown, it struck me that the idea of "Canada" is a very positive one to the Brits. Many people we met invited us to their homes and had we accepted all of the invitations, we would never have accomplished any of our objectives. However, we certainly appreciated all the invitations we received and the kindness we were shown.

The cruiser with which we had entered the canal had been tied up and the boaters were enjoying a tea break.

We finally caught up with them, they had moored their boat amid lush trees in a lagoon, near a lock. As we waved hello to them they called us over to join them for tea and cakes. We rested and chatted with our new friends for more than an hour. Then negotiating the lock together we pressed on for Aldermasten, a few miles further on. We camped out that night, after enjoying our supper and refreshments, at a village pub. The sun was setting as we laid our groundsheets in the thick grass, beside the towpath. Then we crawled into our sleeping bags, we were exhausted yet still excited by the wonderful day we had spent. By eleven p.m. we were in a deep recuperating sleep.

I was awakened by a flashlight shining in my face. Startled I sat up and yelled, "Switch off that light, what the devil's the matter?"

A tall, young man in a navy blue uniform stated in an authoritative voice "You are trespassing on government property, you can't stay here."

"Oh yes, I can," I replied. "This is a public footpath and I have a license to use the canal, leave us alone." The officer I noticed was quite a young man and it was obvious to me in the semi-darkness, that the uniform was not that of the police.

"Who are you?" I asked.

He replied, "I'm with the security staff of the Aldermasten Nuclear Research Centre." And he added "I would like you to come with me to the security centre, and talk to my chief."

I agreed, and accompanied the guard, leaving my brother sleeping. We arrived at the security office and I was introduced to Mr. Jack Smith, head of security in that place. I noticed by the clock on the wall that the time was 4:30 a.m.

"How about a cup of tea?" he asked.

"I'd like that Mr. Smith," I said.

"Call me Jack!" he replied, then to the officer he said, "Do something useful, make us all a cup of tea and some buttered toast."

We were left in the comfortable office sitting in two armchairs. Soon Jack was telling me of his wartime experiences and the role of the Kennet and Avon Canal, as Britain's third line of defense, should the German army invade us. He told me that in 1939 he was a Sergeant Major in charge of a military armory. Guns would be issued to the home guard with which they would practice their marching and rifle handling. The problem was that most of the guns were made of wood as there weren't enough real guns to go round. I forget a lot of the tales he told but he did ask me if I had noticed the small, re-enforced, concrete pill boxes along the canal's banks.

I had noticed those buildings, now Jack said, "Those pill boxes along the canal was Britain's third and final defense. If the "Jerry" took that line, Britain was done for."

Well, by now the sun was coming up and not knowing what to think I bid goodbye to this interesting man. At that time I was anxious to be on my way, however, often in later years I tried to re-establish contact with Jack. In an effort to fill in some of the blanks in his narrative, and I wasn't able to reconnect with him again.

We spent the morning much as the previous day and passed through the lock at Hungerford. Here we tied up for a while and explored this lovely, small town. The canal ran out of water in a few miles and to solve this problem we took the boat onto the nearby road and all three of us, my brother Glyn, the canoe and me, thumbed a ride on a brewery truck. Where in exchange we paid the driver a five pound note. We were driven about ten miles west where water was plentiful again. So we paddled into Newbury. Just east of the lock beside a park, Glyn took off for a rest. I decided to look for the nest of an enormous swan, who I had observed patrolling the canal. This location was like a small lake, with small inlets and clumps of reeds.

Remembering that swans don't attack people I paddled out into the lake despite the hissing and threatening attitude of the enormous cob. Sure enough there a dozen yards from me, was the great cob's wife, nestled in a clump of reeds. Peering ahead trying to spot the contents of the nest, a sudden rush of water and something sharp struck my back. Shocked, I leapt onto a nearby islet and prepared to defend myself from an angry and jealous, thirty pound swan, which now swam to and fro between me and his mate. Don't ever believe that swans are not dangerous. That swan drew blood and ruined a nice white shirt. At a safe moment I fled to safety, picked up Glyn, and once more we continued paddling.

The canal and river were one at this point, entering the lock called for quite a bit of energetic paddling, past the knitting mill on the south bank. There were dozens of young, female factory workers taking their tea break in the sunshine. They cheered us on and were making loud and embarrassing comments to the graying, middle-aged canoeists. We got through the lock with no mishaps and decided to have some rest and refreshments.

Just to the west of the lock the water became a lagoon with several acres in extent. We parked along the south bank where there were perhaps a dozen or more assorted boats. Majority of them were in varying states of disrepair.

I don't think any of them were sailable, maybe they were parked there and used as small cottages. I noticed that though there were signs indicating that fishing and swimming were not allowed, there were quite a number of people engaged in these activities. I suppose it's rather foolish having laws that are pretty well non-enforceable. Mind you, the stuff suspended in that brown, dirty water should have been enough of a deterrent to those sporting Brits.

We continued west enjoying the peace and tranquility of that delightful countryside. What a wonderful holiday, so far as we were making our way along the canal. We stopped at several villages and enjoyed the hospitality of the country pubs. At Marlborough it was market day and the center of town was packed with people.

They were selling and buying produce, small-wares, antiques, etcetera, against a backdrop of the shops and offices of the market square. Much of the architecture was in the Tudor style and freshly painted black and white.

At one end of the square was an interesting old, Roman Catholic Church. At the other end was an Anglican Church that was over four hundred years old. An ancient cast iron sign-post had been erected many years ago at a place on the public way. Hopefully it produced the desired effect on horse abusers. It read:

PLEASE DO NOT INJURE
"A man of kindness to his beast is kind,
A brutal action shoes a brutal mind,
Remember, he who made thee,
made the brute,
Who gave thee speech and reason formed him mute,
He can't complain,
But God's all seeing eye,
Beholds thy cruelty and hears his cry,
He was designed thy servant, not thy drudge,
Remember, his creator is thy judge."

I suppose in those days of passenger and freight traffic on the canal, horses hauling huge loads could be subjected to cruel treatment. We can only hope that the sign was effective. As a matter of interest I did note that the sign was freshly painted and clear of weeds. We stayed nearby at the "Phoenix Hotel," leaving the canoe tied up at the Pewsey Lock.

The next leg of our trip took us to Devizes. The highest point along the system where there is a row of seventeen locks, much like steps descending to the level land below. The locks were at that time (1977) unusable, broken and dry. A group of volunteers were busy at work cleaning up the mess. We made this point the end of our journey west, by boat. We took the boat back to Newbury, by truck and left it in the large shed beside the lock, which was the club-house of the Newbury Canoe Club. We arranged with the club caretaker to rent a little space to park the canoe until one of us returned later that year to pick it up. So we were off, loaded with our traveling equipment to the train station.

Our objective was to arrive in Bristol, then take a bus to Thornbury, which was Glyn's home town. I had really enjoyed spending time on this canoe trip with my brother Glyn and I was feeling sad that were would be parting soon. I would be heading back to Canada and he would be homeward bound to Thornbury. At least we got to catch up and see each other some every few years.

The British Railway guard sent us to the wrong platform, where instead of the slow train to Bristol, we boarded a train heading in a different direction. We discovered our mistake and got off the train as soon as we were able. There we were informed the next train was the following day. I walked down the deserted station towards a signal box. This building was located on stilts about fifteen feet above the ground. In the box through the glass windows I noticed a young man. There were rows of large levers and other equipment for controlling the signal system. Catching his eye he beckoned me up to join him.

Climbing the ladder attached to one of the box supports I joined my host in his workplace. He offered me tea and told me he was an Oxford student reading English Literature. He was glad to have some company. We chatted a while and I told him of our dilemma.

He sympathized and told me he had a solution. The signalman picked up his phone and made contact with the Plymouth express. He told the engine driver he had a couple of people wanting to board. It didn't take long, and within a few minutes the express train stopped at our station. In a few seconds the train was on its way with the two of us on board. We began to wonder if there was anything impossible in this world. We finally arrived in Bristol just in time to board the last bus to Thornbury. We arrived at around 10:30 p.m., just in time to pick up some take-away at the Chinese fish and chip restaurant.

The Wrong Train

My brother Glyn and I were in Newbury, England, and our trip by canoe on the Kennet and Avon Canal was over. What a delightful town Newbury was, and quite near the Canal lock was the boathouse of the Newbury Canoe club. We had planned to travel to Thornbury and I had purchased our train tickets from Newbury to Bristol. The tickets were safely placed in my pocket.

Apparently, we would be in Bristol in time to catch a local bus to Thornbury where our friends would pick us up from the bus stop. The caretaker of the canoe club agreed to look after our canoe and gear until it would be picked up in a month's time. I paid the rental fee and we stashed the little red boat, upside down behind the boathouse.

The railroad station was a couple of miles from the club and it's common knowledge that British railroads usually run on time. So we thought we should hurry to ensure we were at the station for the 6:45 p.m., Bristol Express.

Arriving at the station a minute or two before our train's departure we entered the huge, cavernous area where one train was just coming in and another was leaving. This was the last train to Bristol for that day, so we were a little concerned.

We presented our tickets to the official and asked him which platform was for the Bristol train. "Platform Four," he replied.

The station was very busy and not having time to spare we rushed to platform four where a train was just about to leave. We just made it as the doors of the carriages were being slammed shut and the guard was waving his green flag for the train to depart. Glyn opened a 3rd class carriage door, we entered and I threw our bags in, and closed the door just as the wheels began to turn.

We said goodbye to Newbury, then found two seats and made ourselves comfortable.

Soon the lovely Midland countryside began to slide past. England is such a beautiful country. Our carriage was crowded, and several children were playing about. We were occupying two seats which included four places much like a club car.

There was a table between us and the seats in front of us, were occupied by two little girls, whose mom and dad were in the seats across the aisle.

Such a lot of friendly people and as the train swayed along to the music of the clicking rails, we all became quite friendly. I have no idea what we talked about but somewhere in the conversation we mentioned that we had travelled by canoe to Newbury. The children wanted to hear all about our adventure. Then maybe an hour or so into our train-ride the girls said they were going home to Plymouth after a holiday with their Granny.

Ouch! "Glyn," I said, "We are on the wrong train."

By then we were informed that the train we were on was the Express to Plymouth with a stop at Ashby de la Zouch and Exeter. Obviously, the ticket collector in Newbury had misdirected us. Between us we discussed the intelligence of that employee, and his lineage, and how in his ignorance he had caused us to be in this predicament.

Then we realized there was no point but to make the best of it. Soon in the darkening evening, we stopped at Ashby de la Zouch. We got off the train. Before we had a chance to close the carriage door, the whistle blew and the train was on its way.

The one platform of this small station seemed so derelict.

We wondered what we were going to do. We talked about walking into the town, but had no idea how far away it was and by now it was starting to get dark. There was one lonely light, which cast eerie shadows on the deserted, lonely place. Glyn then pointed to a small raised building about a hundred yards away from the platform. We could see the interior which was well lit and a man seemed to be there, moving around.

"I'll talk to him," I said.

I walked to the end of the platform, while Glyn stayed with our bags. There we could see a small structure, built on supporting legs about twelve feet above the ground. This was the control center for changing the rails, to send trains safely on their way. In the center of the room was a row of shiny brass levers which the operator would use. The man on duty was seated wearing a headset and reading a book. As he got up to operate one of the controls he spotted me looking up, and beckoned for me to climb up the ladder and visit with him. It didn't take long and I found myself in this cozy, warm control area with this very friendly young man.

A "cup of tea?" was his greeting. The book he had been reading I noticed was a collection of Chaucer's poems.

He smiled at my expression and said, "I'm a student at Oxford, reading English Lit."

He told me a little about his part-time job and how he would receive instructions about which levers to pull. I told him of our predicament and how we had been misdirected and ended up on the wrong train.

"Don't worry about that, we'll have that sorted out in a minute," he said in a conversational manner.

He proceeded to make a phone call and an interesting conversation took place. Our new friend was talking to the train engineer. He was asking about the express train that was due to come through the station, on its way to Bristol. It was not scheduled to stop but he convinced the driver to stop for a few seconds, to allow two travelers aboard, who would be very grateful for his help. The train driver had mentioned that he was a couple of minutes ahead of schedule and that he could make up for lost time.

A few minutes later the train squealed to a pause in that pokey, little, darkened station and in less than four seconds we were aboard. The door was slammed shut and we returned a goodbye wave to our thoughtful helper.

The engine driver blew two short toots on the train whistle as if to say, "So there, we will be on way now."

An hour or so later we arrived at Bristol. The bus was waiting and we continued along our journey and made it to Thornbury, just in time to be served at 'Choy's Fish and Chips' for our supper. We walked to our friend's house with a spring in our step while eating our fish and chips out of the newspaper wrappings. It was a satisfactory end to an exciting day. The thought passed through my mind, if you ask for help in the appropriate way, it usually arrives.

It struck me that the question I asked the official about "The Bristol Train" could mean either the train going to Bristol, or the train coming from Bristol. And in hindsight, I might have caused the situation by not being clear with my question.

Gone Fishing

One of my favorite places to be is St. Petersburg, Florida. More than two million people make their homes in the Tri-city area of Tampa, Clearwater and St. Petersburg. I love to fish in the rich, warm, salt-water which surrounds the peninsula. Whose, glorious, sunshine and silver-gold beaches make this place feel like a paradise. Our second home was on the Island of Coquina Key and whenever possible my wife and I, with our five children would flee Ontario's bitter cold and enjoy a respite under Florida's warm, blue sky. We loved our time to-gether, when the kids were small they'd accompany me to the fishing piers. It was where we'd try our luck, though often we'd be accused of feeding the fishes and pelicans. It didn't really matter as it was the effort rather than results that gave us the most pleasure.

I purchased extra fishing rods for the children though they refused to impale the shrimp-bait on their hooks. I eventually tired of baiting for them and was not unhappy as one by one, they decided to leave their fishing rods at home. They did however, continue to accompany us to the piers and play in the warm waters of the Gulf certainly, within our view.

We had driven from our house on the Key and found a convenient parking space right beside the entrance to the pier. We had decided to try our luck at this southernmost point of what is known as "the Beaches." The tide had turned and the high water hid most of the gold-en, sandy beach. Sea oats had been planted just above the high-water mark and the low dunes at the top of the beach, had been planted with astonishing success. This three-foot, lush, golden grass made a lovely wind-break for those sunbathing in its lee.

We all marched down the rocky path and onto the old concrete

pier. Several elderly men were fishing there; some had favorite spots and
some of these old anglers were loathe
to share this public space. Bait buckets
and other gear was secured for security's
sake. As we came close I noticed that the
fishermen spread themselves about the
piers-end to make it more difficult for
a late-comer to find some space. Having
noticed the subtle maneuvers, I stopped
short of the popular point and prepared
my place, fifteen yards from the closest,
occupied spot. In reality fishing is a sport
whose success depends to a great extent
on chance. I felt that success was depen-

dant on patience and luck rather than skill and location.

I cast my line into the flowing tide; nearby my wife and children at
play. The men on the pier were continuing to fish. I thought I detected
the occasional sly glance in my direction. The sea's undulating surface
hypnotically attracting me. I quickly noticed a variety of flotsam floating past me. Suddenly, about thirty feet from where I stood, I noticed
that a light-green rectangular, small piece of paper floated on the surface. It was almost hidden by the twinkling of the sun's reflection from
the tiny wavelets. In disbelief I stared and hastily wound in my reel,
sure enough a U.S. treasury bill, obviously saturated and somewhat
bleached, was slowly floating past. I cast my line over the note, directly
across its center and as the weight of the lure sank, it drew the line
down. The sodden bill folded onto itself, with the nylon line securely
entrapping it.

Carefully, I reeled in my prize and as I retrieved the note, I observed
that my luck had been noticed by several of the elderly anglers on the
pier. A tiny, wizened, walnut-colored man in a straw hat and dirty
white shorts, with the thinnest legs I had ever seen, came over to where
I stood. He advised me that he had dropped a banknote earlier and
claimed my prize as his own.

"What was its denomination?" I asked. "Um, Um," the old chap hesi-
tated. "A Ten," he finally said.

"Sorry, wrong number" I smiled at him.

Two other old codgers tried their scam, both guessing the wrong number. I folded my gear and we prepared to leave. As I left with my wife and kids to have an early supper at "Morrison's," I called out as I waved goodbye.

"It was a hundred, see you boys tomorrow." I patted my breast pocket where the twenty dollar bill was drying nicely. We got into our car and made our way toward our home.

It was still a little early for supper so the kids agreed that I could try for a few minutes on the pier on 49th street. This was a wooden structure a few yards from the highway. A dozen or so people were trying their luck. I found a spot, not too crowded and cast my line into the green, flowing tide. Within minutes a lot of shouting, screaming and noisy commotion came from just a few yards from where I stood.

"Oye, Oye, help, help me," a tiny scarecrow of an elderly lady was screaming that her husband had been drinking and had fallen into the water and he couldn't swim.

It took me five or six seconds to haul in my line and I leapt to the corner of the pier, where he had been standing. I leaned over the pier and could just make out the form of a brightly colored shirt, a couple of feet below the murky green surface of the water. Its depth was about twenty five feet at that point. I grabbed my gaff, then lowered myself over the edge of the pier. I kept a firm grip onto the metal safety fence. The old lady all the while screaming for help and holding onto my shirt.

It didn't take more than a minute or two for my thrashing gaff to secure a hold onto the old chap's shirt. I quickly brought him up to the surface and into the hands of other would-be helpers. Thank God that's over I thought as I made my way off the pier toward our car. Again, I was caught by the same old lady who clutched my shirt.

"Don't go," she said.

I stopped, turned and smiled down at her, expecting a word of thanks, "Your husband's fine now," I said.

To my surprise, the old lady looked up into my face, her tiny, beady eyes glinting and she angrily shouted, "His glasses, they were new, they came off in the water, why didn't you get them?"

A Small Business

"I don't believe you," Fred looked at me with his mouth partly open, "Surely that's against the law, even in St. Petersburg."

"No, no, Fred," I assured him, "It didn't happen every day, or night in this case." I didn't know whether to call the police or just stay and watch the show. If I called the police would they think I was some old duffer wasting their time, when mayhem was going on down the road? What could I complain about? Someone operating a business without a license? This action was taking place on our street, at two o'clock in the morning. Yes, and out of the back of an old Kingswood Estate Chevy station wagon."

Coquina Key is an island of about a square mile in total, located in Tampa Bay and was part of St. Petersburg's, South Side. The Key was a grand place to live where it's mostly black people living in harmony with the white population. The strip of water between the island and the mainland peninsula, seemed to create a barrier. This protected the residents from the dangers and crime, which was happening on a regular basis in that area of St. Petersburg.

On this particular night, Kay and I had gone to bed around midnight, as usual, and were awakened about two a.m., by some giggling and music being played in a big station wagon.

The vehicle was parked in front of our house under the street lamp. We lay in bed listening to the congenial noises which were just a bit too loud to allow us to go back to sleep. Looking through the slats covering our window, we could see what was going on. It seemed like an old black and white movie, with the action observed through the dappled shadows of a night-time tropical scene.

The muted conversations and laughter were not offensive but occasionally there would be shoving and shouts of complaint. There was a line of several young, black men, dressed in rough jeans and t-shirts waiting for their turn to climb into the back of the wagon and do their thing.

We watched the scene for a while slightly fascinated by this unusual action. A young black man stood at the rear entrance of the wagon who seemed to be in charge of collecting the fee. I have no idea what price was charged, but I did have the impression that the amount was negotiable. After the deal was made the customer would remove his jeans and climb into the rear of the car.

While the client was getting his money's worth the waiting line of customers, maybe five or six, would be joking and kibitzing around. Sometimes even punching on the side of the car telling the occupants to hurry. Then, when the client would leave the car, he would slip on his pants and be on his way.

The transaction would repeat itself every few minutes. We noticed that the line remained about constant in its length as other boys and youths would appear out of the shadows and join the line. It was as if drawn by some invisible thread. It struck me at the time, what system would determine the paternity of any unfortunate pregnancy? DNA was in its infancy but who cared anyway?

Coquina Key was patrolled by a police cruiser once every three hours. I recall one night our island was searched for some escaped prisoner. The police helicopter, with searchlights and loudspeakers, like a powerful gunship, located the escapee, bringing him to earth, in the mangrove swamp on the other side of the park.

The police force was very efficient but somehow, a few minutes before the arrival of the cruiser on its rounds, the carnival across the road closed up shop and drove off. Leaving those behind, maybe disappointed as they took off in different directions. The night's work in Whiting Drive was done and no doubt the entrepreneurs found a place to do more business in some other part of the city.

What an idea. A mobile brothel. A knocking shop on wheels. God help us. At least twelve shared their body fluids that night.

Watching the news report the other day two social workers were discussing the spread of S.T.D., and made a comment that more than half the teen-age population had some sort of sexually transmitted disease. The idea of abstinence seems to be repugnant even though many afflicted people will die an awful death. While the young man and woman were closing down their shop, I noticed that the girl looked to be about sixteen and the man in his early twenties. They seemed to be dividing the spoils then jumping into their vehicle, they drove quietly off into the night.

We returned to Canada a week later and in that time, at least, there was no repeat of this sort of happening. At least outside our house in St. Pete.

Those Damn Mocking Birds

Where we lived on Coquina Key, there were a lot of mocking birds. We loved to watch them in their neat, trim, grey suits. They always seemed so smart hopping around doing what birds do. Sometime in the early mornings, the plentiful wildlife sang their leaderless concert to the joy of anyone within listening distance.

Now our neighbor, Ray, felt quite different. He hated those damn mocking birds. Ray was a retired military officer and an engineer. In his seventies, he was an avid gardener. His back yard is where he cultivated bananas. Florida is not famous for bananas. However, Ray had nurtured those fruit and his huge, lush plants, through careful husbandry, they thrived and produced very nice fruit of the "ladyfinger" variety.

The occasional frost was the enemy, and smoke pots and spraying water were his weapons to fight that foe. Whoever heard of growing pomegranates in Pinellas County? No one! Ray produced his pomegranates from two small trees, which were his pride and joy. He presented us with two choice fruits, which though difficult to eat were sweet and juicy. As a child I would eat a pomegranate half, using a pin to pick out the seeds and eating them one by one.

As it happened, black figs were Ray's favorite fruit. They were also the favorite fruit of those damn mocking birds. At almost any time of the year you can buy figs at the grocery store. I guess the taste of the fruits of your labor is infinitely better. He provided warmth, water and food for his plants and protected them from predators by draping a fine net over the plants. It didn't matter what Ray did, each ripening fig was stolen by his nemesis.

Often I've heard our next door neighbor cursing when he found his fruit had vanished. He would set his alarm and get up at first light only to discover he was a few minutes too late.

It was my habit to get up before dawn and have a cup of tea in the Florida room. This room overlooked Ray's backyard, then later I'd go back to bed.

One of the funniest sights was to see Ray, at the crack of dawn, creep out of his house, dressed in his boiler-suit underwear and a woolen toque. Often the rear flap would be undone. He was a single man in his seventies, heavily built, with an enormous belly. Bald as a coot, and with an air rifle in his hands waiting to get a shot at those damn birds. Suddenly you'd see him lift the gun and fire a shot which would miss by yards. His eyesight was bad and his shaking arms were ensuring the quarry's survival.

Around that time Ray brought home a lady and from that time on he lost interest in his garden. Within no time at all there were wedding bells ringing in the air. The house was sold and they moved into a condo, in Clearwater. The plants died off, and our mocking birds, deprived of the exotic fruits, returned to their usual diet, elsewhere.

Even though Ray was only a few years my senior, I felt toward him as if he was a favorite uncle or a big brother. It's a funny thing how you can completely lose touch, how easy friendship can fail unless it's nurtured. A year or two passed. And I missed his wisdom and humor, so wrote him a letter to rekindle what had been a pleasing friendship. His brief reply included his hope that I would visit him on my next trip to Florida.

That fall, of 1998, I did see him in that small, neat as a pin condo. There was none of Ray's fishing gear hanging around. No cooking pots and pans were visible as was the usual mess associated with a happy bachelor's life. There was none of those exotic smells of an elderly man testing out his creative cooking skills.

I watched Ray and his new appendage as close as a third arm. Perhaps she was just waiting for two jovial, elderly men to use an unacceptable cuss word, so as she could frown her disapproval.

I did notice neatly placed around the condo walls, several strategically placed pictures of Jesus, Mary and other sacred symbols, and crosses in the entry hall. We sat for a while on the new furniture, covered in throws to keep it clean. We missed those old, warm and comfortable chairs we sat on in the old house in St. Pete.

The biggest change appeared in my old friend Ray. His appearance was the same, maybe a few years older and a few less pounds, but gone was his fun-filled humor. His cheerful exuberant conversation and his boisterous laugh had disappeared. I felt an awful sadness for the fate of that poor, dear, old man, struck down in his senior prime, by the most lethal, lingering weapon of all. Stuck in an unsuitable marriage.

I was with my friend for nearly two hours before I left for home. We did talk some about the good old times on Coquina Key. I noticed only one plant in the place, a potted fern, and not a spot of ground for Ray to play the gardener. He was seventy seven that fall, a physically strong, old man now it seemed, waiting day by day to reach the end of his trail. Unfortunately, he was not overly concerned whether it was to be next year or next week.

Lake Maggiore - 1995

St. Petersburg, Florida, is probably the one city which has everything going for it. Great climate, beaches, shopping, golf courses, wonderful parks, and marinas, etc. It also has an abundance of flora and fauna to add to its fabulous interest. I have traveled to many countries in the course of my work. I must say that the Department of Parks and the Department of Leisure Services, in St. Petersburg, provide the citizens, of this friendly city, the most excellent services, for their allocation of taxes.

All across the city, areas have been set aside for the use of the public. There are many water-front beaches, parks and marinas, beautifully maintained, clean and tidy. Many of these facilities are free to the public. When a charge is required it is invariably modest.

From our home on Coquina Key it was about a fifteen minute walk to Lake Maggiore on 4th Street South, in St. Pete. Strolling along the lake-side, you could enjoy watching the egrets fishing in the shallows. I love to feel the gentle breezes flowing through the reeds which, were growing along the shore. Coots, pelicans and assorted ducks are permanent residents here. The lake flows through the lovely park by the South entrance.

Swimming in the lake is not recommended. Large signs had been erected around the lake, warning of its dangers. Lurking around the shallows of the lake, large alligators, warming themselves in the sunshine, were the subject of the warnings. Dogs playing amongst the reeds and in the shallow water, would occasionally be swallowed, by what first appeared to be a rotten log, floating in the water.

Lakeside Park contained a public library with a small exhibit of the local flora and fauna. This was a very popular facility which was used as a learning center for young children, from the schools in the area. Often when we would exchange our library books there, we could watch the children with their teachers, engaged in a learning experience. Listening to the chatter and excitement of the children was a treat which we found very pleasing.

The large glass doors of the library had been treated in order that you could look through the glass from within, but not the other way round. When it was not busy you could stand just inside the door and watch the antics of the raccoons scrounging in the refuse bins, outside the doors. The parking areas were quite extensive and were shaded with great, Florida Cedars, Loblolly Pines, Oaks and Shrubs. The numerous Royal Palms growing in the park and the manicured footpaths, made this an attractive place to spend a pleasant hour. Hanging from the many trees, masses of Spanish moss added to the charming atmosphere.

On this particular day, the warm spring sun shone from a cloudless, blue sky. My wife and I planned a leisurely, afternoon stroll through the park. We parked the car in a shaded area and began our walk along the pathway. This would bring us past a small pond filled with dirty, drainage water. The pond was actually a sink-hole which was in the process of being filled in with dirt and vegetation. It was probably about four feet deep and sixty feet across. Strolling ahead of us along the path was a young woman, with her small boy following along behind her, on his little tricycle. As they were meandering along, the small child had gradually trailed further and further away from his mom. All of a sudden I saw about twenty feet from the little boy, an enormous alligator, lying on the grass, in the sun. It was not more than eight feet from where the child would pass in just a few seconds.

I was shocked for a second, and concerned for the little boy and ourselves. Then, armed with my walking stick, I ran, shouting to the mother to look out for the little boy, and shaking my stick at the alligator. The boy who became alarmed, ran down the path to his mother, right past the gator. I again shouted warnings to the mother, who as yet had not noticed the huge animal. She swept the boy up into her arms and began to abuse me for frightening her child. By this time I was shaking with fright. Very quickly the mother and child were getting into their car and soon leaving the park.

As fast as I could run, I made my way to the park gate where there was a small office, manned by the park staff. I called for help and after a few minutes a young park attendant in uniform asked me how she could be of help. Almost incoherent, I managed to explain what had transpired and my fear that some other child might be in danger.

A young, handsome co-worker had joined us from the office. He was very laid-back considering what I thought to be a crisis situation. The two park attendants looked at each other for a minute or two, when the young man drawled with a pleasant, southern accent,

"Was that a gator about eight feet long lying out beside the sink-hole pond?"

"Yes, yes," I replied. "If you come quickly I'll show you."

Smiling, with such a perfect set of white teeth, the worker assured me. "You all don't have to worry sir, gators don't eat often, and that old boy Charlie, ate a possum last Saturday."

And that's all I'm going to say about that remark!

Arf Arf, Woof Woof, Grrrr...

The sound of a barking dog can eventually drive a man mad. Like the Chinese water torture or being forced to sleep with your eyes open. Systematic and continuous noise for one, is often unheard by the dog-fancier. How is it that the owner of the barking dog doesn't hear the grating, abrasive noise, when the neighbors suffer lack of sleep waiting for the tuneless noise to stop?

Ray needed his sleep, however, for several nights in a row the neighbor across the park had let the dog out before she went to bed, for the night. The persistent calling for entry to the dog owner's home had met with no welcoming opened door. The continual barking for some reason was not heard by the dog's owner who was the closest to its source.

A kind and gentle man, even the most sensitive animal lover can eventually reach the point of saturation, when he is at the end of his tether, for further torment. Ray had tried closing his windows. Putting his head under the pillow. He had tried extra drinks and ear-plugs. Nothing worked for my friend to keep at bay the grinding, cursed sounds, "arf arf, woof, woof." How can any creature keep barking for so many hours at a time? How can the dog's owner ignore the penetrating, blasphemous cacophony?

This was my first night's loss of sleep. I was tired when I arrived from up north and my hope for a refreshing sleep had been interrupted by the barking dog. From Ray, I had learned that the dog being let out at night was a recent happening. It was the fifth night in a row that Ray had his sleep ruined by the dog. I was sitting enjoying the early sunrise, having a cup of tea, watching the morning news broadcast on t.v, when suddenly there was the sound of my friend slamming his front door. I peered through the sheers covering the window. I could see Ray marching across our front lawn, he looked angry and I could hear him calling for some quiet.

"I'll kill the bastard" he shouted.

Ray was dressed in a pair of shorts and a thick sweater stretched tight across his enormous belly. He was a very big man in his mid-seventies. A nice and gentle man despite his military background. He wore a toque and slippers. As he crossed the lawn I could hear him shout to Tom, the other Neighbor.

"Tom, hey Tom, are you there? That blasted dog, I've had enough. Have you got your gun? I'll shoot the bastard."

There was silence for a minute or two.

"Thanks Tom, is it loaded? With ten shells you say, that should do it. Now I can get some peace and quiet."

The entire conversation was expressed at high volume, and was intended to be overheard by the owner of the dog.

The strident scream of an upset older lady rang through the air.

"Don't you dare come over here and hurt my dog, he's done nothing wrong, dogs bark, it's only natural."

Getting into the spirit of things Ray called out "I'll be right over, don't take the dog into the house now, it's too late for that, I'll go in after him, I'll get the bastard."

The voice came back "I know who you are now, you're Ray Barnett and I've called the police, they will be here in a minute and they'll stop you from hurting Bruno."

With that we heard a police cruiser squealing his wheels round the corner and come skidding to a halt on our front driveway. The young, muscular policeman jumped out of the squad car. He was drawing his revolver as he called out, "You, drop your gun and raise your arms, you're under arrest."

Tom did not have a gun to lend Ray, the gun talk had been a ruse and meant to scare the dog owner. As far as the officer was concerned a gun had been part of the transaction and he had no intention of getting hurt. Threats of armed violence had been made and this was a crime, even in St. Petersburg, Florida. "Lie on the ground with your hands behind your back," demanded the policeman.

Ray is a heavy man, a retired military officer and engineer. He had heard the policeman in total disbelief' and he didn't move. As it seemed to the cop that he was resisting arrest, he called on his radio for back-up. In less than two minutes another squad-car hurtled onto the scene. All the while I was watching this drama unfold, right in our front yard.

The second officer joined his colleague and together they tried to subdue our friend. Ray weighed maybe two hundred and fifty pounds with legs like tree-trunks. He just stood there passively resisting and the two young cops were unable to throw him to the ground. He didn't fight back, he just stood there rigid and refused to fall.

After a few minutes, in desperation the first cop called for further back-up and within a couple of minutes a third cruiser with a sergeant and a constable squealed onto the scene. And between them they were able to cart my friend off to jail. For some strange reason the dog had ceased barking and in a few minutes the dust had settled and the neighborhood assumed its usual Sunday morning tranquility.

We spent an uneasy morning. Tom came over from next door and suggested we go down to the police station and come to Ray's aid. Really, what could we do? Everyone in our area, with the exception of Bruno's mother, felt sorry for dear old Ray. He was always so generous with his citrus and bananas. Kids making a short-cut through his yard were never reported, a growl and a yell would scare them off for a while.

There didn't seem to be any justice remaining in this world. At seventy five years old, Ray being taken away by four policemen for shouting at the old biddies' dog to stop it from barking. Of course, the police having a complaint from a citizen that a neighbor had threatened her dog, with a weapon, were obliged to take action and that they did. The only thing we could do for Ray was to have some cash ready in case he might need bail money.

It was around two in the afternoon when a chastened Ray was driven to his house in a cab. He quietly entered his little bungalow and shut the door. He remained unseen for most of the day. It seemed a bit odd in a way as it was a glorious, sunny, afternoon.

The kind of day that drew most folks outdoors to the beach or for other fun, outdoor activities. Florida is all about having fun on the beach. Not on this particular Sunday did Ray feel up to his usual self. While I was gathering some grapefruit from our garden, I did see Ray for a few minutes while he was picking some tomatoes from his garden for his supper. I waved to him and he acknowledged my greeting and waved back but did not stop to chat.

The next day, Monday, he was up early and waiting outside for a cab. I had never seen Ray dressed like that, blazer, white shirt and a tie, grey slacks and shiny, black shoes. At first I wondered who it was. I was up and about and stepped out of our front door.

"Good morning Ray" I called out. "Have you got time for a coffee?"

"Later Trev" he replied "Right now I've got to see a man about a dog." A taxi arrived and whisked him away.

Well, it was late that afternoon when Ray came over to our place for coffee. He looked like his old self in his shorts, T-shirt and sandals. We sat in the Florida room out of the hot sun drinking our coffee while I encouraged Ray to tell us what happened this morning.

"You see I was told to be at the magistrates office at nine this morning, he said matter of factly. "It's always a good idea to dress properly for that type of meeting." He took a long drink from his coffee and settled back in his chair.

"I had to answer to a charge of threatening bodily harm with a weapon, there were other charges too, such as resisting arrest and disturbing the peace. Hell Trev, I'm 75 years old, I am a law-abiding citizen and a proud American veteran, with medals to prove it. I don't owe a dime in this world. There was no gun, and there never was.

I then explained to the magistrate, "It was the blasted dog who was disturbing the peace, not me."

"We chatted a while about a number of things and it turned out that he didn't like barking dogs either. He gave me a warning to keep the peace, and that was that."

It was after five o'clock and the sun was beginning to cool down. Time to invite our neighbor Tom to join us and crack open a fresh bottle of vodka. The three of us sat and watched the sun go down as we enjoyed our drinks. We used our own fresh-squeezed limes and as we mellowed out we began to see aspects of the case which caused us some merriment. Especially the part about it taking four, young, strong men, St Petersburg's finest, to arrest our elderly pal.

Molly

While at our place on Coquina Key in St. Petersburg, break-ins and mayhem were regular fare. Molly lived alone most of the time and the neighbors looked out for her.

Molly was an eighty-year-old widow from up north. She was small, frail and innocent. One day, Ray, the next door neighbor, gave her a pistol as protection. It looked so real and the trick was to leave it out in plain sight, on the coffee table. Suppose a crook was casing the place, at a glance they could see that the home occupant was armed and ready for business. That would be a deterrent so he could ply his nefarious games elsewhere.

The ruse seems to have worked, as in the ten years that Molly was there, no crook ever bothered her. Ray's instructions were to the effect that it was always a good idea when a robber is caught in the act of doing his nasty deeds, to allow him to be inside the house if you kill him. If you shoot him prematurely, too early, and his body is outside the house, when the police arrive, you will be arrested for murder and for using excessive force. Surely that can't be true?

There was an odd story on the news around that time. A liquor store in Miami had been broken into several times over the last six months. The police had been of no help in dealing with this series of crimes. The frustrated owner devised a plan. Access to his property had been through a sky-light in the roof so he suspended a net of chicken-wire just below where the crook had entered. For an extra jolt he had connected the trap to the electric system, then he went about his business. In his line of work, trade was brisk.

A few days later on the evening news it was announced that a liquor-store owner in Miami had been arrested and charged with first degree homicide. It was an open and shut case. The intruder had entered the store through the sky-light and fell into the wire net. He had been electrocuted, the shock had caused the man to have a heart attack, from which he succumbed.

The charge of first degree murder was made and the store-keeper was arrested. Bail was disallowed and the man was held in custody awaiting his trial. Frustrated customers had to find their way to another liquor store two blocks away.

Half the population began to protest that the police should not have arrested the shop-keeper. There is a concept of private property and everyone has the right to protect themselves. On the other hand, the cruel owner of the liquor store used vicious force which caused the unfortunate entrant to die prematurely. Needless to say, the matter coalesced into two camps. The media was taking up the cause of the dead man. While the more conservative side vehemently declared that the shopkeeper was innocent of any wrong-doing.

Crime is rife in Florida and the courts are very busy. It was nearly a year before the accused's case was to be heard. The civil liberty people had a field day, constantly harping on how the poor were treated so unfairly and how rife with bigotry was the law and legal system. The poor dead man was apparently a gentleman from south of the border. The accused's case was scheduled to be heard thirteen months after the event. As a consequence, the accused, and according to tradition was "innocent until proven guilty." He had already been punished by assumption.

As might have been expected, the trial was a long and difficult one. For whatever reason, the public prosecutor felt it was his duty to obtain a conviction whatever the price and the media made it obvious where its sympathy lay. The defense, however, was able to argue successfully and after several weeks the defendant was found "not guilty."

There was an interesting and similar happening in Toronto around that time. There had been a proliferation of "corner stores" also known as "convenience stores" in the province. Often these stores were managed by men and women from a variety of Asian countries. These citizens often worked up to sixteen hours a day to make a decent living. Strangely, these little stores were often the target of robbers. A thief, later described as a young Asian male, entered the store armed with a machete. After knocking the cashier to the ground, wielding his machete he demanded money from the manager. All this was happening quickly. Then the crook grabbed a handful of money from the till, kicked the body on the floor and fled.

Not to be used thus, the owner ran after the fleeing thief and after a short chase, tackled him to the ground. The storekeeper was able to subdue the thief and dragged him back to the store and locked him in the store room and called 911.

Oddly, the police arrested the storekeeper for kidnapping and forcible confinement. Later the public's clamorous response to the absurd action of the police was able to convince the Crown to release the store owner and not proceed with the charges. Later the robber was charged and taken off to jail.

The hero of the incident was later lauded for his courageous actions.

The Panhandler

The last glimmer of wintry sunlight filtered into the narrow, dusty lane. The bundle of rags in the doorway stirred. The lined, whisker-stubbled face of the old outcast slowly unfolded from the pile. Peering into the shadows, he was blinking rapidly to clear his rheumy eyes. At the same moment an empty wine bottle escaped from among the rags, clattering down the steps, from the doorway to the pavement below.

The man's eyes twitched to the bottle as he lurched to his feet, his worn cap slipped sideways, as he clutched wildly for the bottle and missed. Stumbling down the three steps from his doorway refuge, a whisper of the cold night air tormented his shrunken frame. He gathered his clothes more closely around his body.

Casting the last remains of drugged sleep from his sore eyes, he passed his crisp jacket cuff across his toothless mouth. Then he picked up the bottle, blinked and carefully examined its contents. He unscrewed the cap and lifted the empty bottle shakily to his eager lips. A few last drops spilled onto his dry tongue. Smacking his parched lips he returned the bottle to the gutter.

Shaking as the cold wind bit through his threadbare rags, he rearranged the newspapers stuffed into his clothes. The papers secured his warmth against the gathering night. Deep in his subconscious, vague memories of better times struggled against his present needs. His thoughts turned to his most serious problem, to get the cash for a bottle of "Seventy Four," before the cut-rate liquor store closed at ten.

At one time this man had been employed, had a wife and home, and was a paid-up member of society. Gradually, over the years his use of liquor had gained immense importance in his life. Anger, acrimony and drunkenness caused the deterioration of his family relationships. With a final curse he left the home of caring and sharing, to one which was to satisfy his loathsome craving. His needs were few, some food, a place to rest and a daily dose of wine or spirits. At first part-time jobs were available then as the needs were more demanding, it took more time to get the cash required. Without noticing the changes he sank lower into the depths of addiction. Until now he was reduced to his daily ritual, begging and scrounging for the price of a bottle.

He searched again through his threadbare clothes, not a single dime, not a chance to earn the cost of the bottle. Muttering to himself he turned and sought the main street of this small, Virginian town.

Flecks of snow dusted the almost deserted main street. The store windows reflected a hope for Christmas. Without a thought or a glance to the shop-fronts wonderland, he looked for a chance to appease his urgent need. A well-dressed man approached, muffled against the cold night air. His footsteps were firm and friendly, his arms laden with cheerful packages. The outcast seemed to shake himself and assumed a more presentable appearance. An apologetic half-smile crinkled the lines about his eyes. His left shoulder hunched a little high, with his right hand slightly clawed toward him and with a tearful catch in his strained, hoarse voice.

He said softly, "Bless you Sir, could you be helping an unfortunate man with the price of a bed for the night?"

The facial expression of the shopper had been almost smiling as his thoughts were of his two children and his beautiful wife at home. His one thought had been his family and how much he loved them. His hurrying steps had been homeward, where he could help in the final preparations for the holiday. Midnight mass drew the little family closer together as they thanked God for their happy life.

Friends had told him he worked too hard, maybe that was true but the rewards were so high. He had gained the respect of his colleagues at work and his recent promotion to area manager was evidence of his success. His increased income made it possible for him to be really extravagant. This Christmas the thought of the small package, with its brightly colored wrapping that contained the gold necklace that his wife had always wanted. He was excited about the thought of her opening the gift and her smiling eyes, added haste to his homeward step.

The young man heard the outcast's appeal and normally would have brushed aside the whining plea, however, Christmas Eve is a time for forgiveness and love. His thoughts for an instant returned to the time, when he was only six years old and his own father had deserted him and his mother, with his tiny sister. How they had struggled for many years to make a better life.

Here was a despicable drunk, smelling of cheap wine and dirt. He was torn between the Christmas spirit and the unhappy memory. He stared at the old man standing there on the sidewalk. He knew that in his wallet was a ten dollar bill and some loose change, his comfortable home was just a few minutes away. His shopping was done. Here in front of him the beggar stood his arm clawed forward in expectant hope. Quietly, he knew what he should do, no questions, no recrimination. He took his wallet from his pocket and put the remaining cash into the outstretched hand.

The old derelict's eyes lit up, his grateful thanks and bless you sir followed the young man down the street. He walked for just a few more yards when suddenly a thought flashed into his mind. He mulled over the idea to take the old man home and have him join them for a few hours of warmth and ease. He turned and his eyes swept the snow dusted sidewalk, there was no sign of the old man. He stood still for a few moments about to continue on his way when an old, ragged, man came out of the nearby Cut Rate Liquor Store. He was clutching to his chest a large, brown paper bag.

He stared at the man, hardly able to believe his eyes. He had given his last cash to the drunk in hope of giving him a taste of kindness and some Xmas cheer. Then again he thought he should have taken him home. What a fool, he thought to himself and turned once more his footsteps firmly homeward. He felt deep inside, an edge of guilt.

The beggar's steps were hasty and aimed toward the narrow lane that wasn't that far away. There, as the night fell round that sleepy town, and the last happy preparations were being made for the tomorrow's festive cheer. He planned to return to his favorite spot. All bundled up in his ragged clothes, he would enjoy the fruits of his begging. Not a thought for that generous man who had so freely given all that he had to spare.

An almost smile creased the thin lips as he stepped off the sidewalk, eager to test the Xmas gift. The bag of liquor at his chest impaired his view, as he stepped into the path of a hurrying cab. His last memory, as he fell to the ground was the sound of splintering glass as his parcel was stricken from his arms and crashed to the ground. The cab screeched to a halt and the driver jumped out. He was bending over the old man's body and he could see that he was badly hurt and ran back to his car and called for help.

The young man who had helped the drunk, heard the crash of splintering glass. Instinctively he knew who the victim was. He turned and hurried to the main street where the crash had taken place. There on the cold street the old man lay with a few people gathering around. In the distance you could hear the sound of the siren as the ambulance rushed to the accident scene. Just a few minutes was all it took. The medics and the police quickly did their job. Within twenty minutes only the broken glass and the lingering smell of drink indicated that an accident had taken place.

The hospital alerted to the victim's needs and took care of his injuries. His arm and leg were broken and the fractures were set and he was admitted and made comfortable between clean and welcoming sheets. The sedation was taking effect and the old man slept amongst the Gods, for the first time in many years. With one last look the young, well-dressed, man who had gone to the cottage hospital, continued home to his wife and two small children. He told them the details of the incident, which left the poor old beggar in such a miserable state. Again, he thought he could have prevented the old man's suffering if only he had obeyed his first Christian impulse. There in the warmth and love of the family they changed into their Sunday clothes. They were going to meet their friends at Saint Penelope's Church, two short blocks away.

Christmas was a few days past. The family was happy and content. Their hopes fulfilled. Dad was back at work and next week Billie the oldest would be back at school. Six years old and already he was showing promise.

Last week's local paper lay on the desk, the bottom of the front page reported the accident. The manager once again read the unpleasant details. "I'll visit him on Sunday," he promised himself.

After church, he visited the hospital. In the ward where the old man lay, the young man introduced himself to the injured man.

"I'm Jack Wilson," he said. Cleaned and shaved and a few days without booze had made a difference to the old gent's looks.

"I'm John," he replied as he took the offered hand. He sat and chatted for a while and the injured man said "You look familiar, but I can't think where."

Jack explained they had met a few minutes before the accident but thought it better not to give the details. He said goodbye, promising he would come to see him again.

The following Sunday Jack noticed that John seemed more spry and was moving around with the aid of a pair of hospital crutches. The first few days had been the worst. The terrible need for drink and the pain of his injuries had made him frantic. Only the drugs had kept him under control. The doctors had told him he could soon go home. "Where's that?" he had asked, of course there was no reply.

Jack had told his wife about the visits and an idea which stuck in his mind. "How would it be if we brought him home for a few days, the change would do him good? And he has to leave the hospital soon."

At first the protests were loud and strong. Gradually she changed her mind and finally agreed. They put a small bed in the sewing room of their house, just in case.

Jack brought the old man home a few days later, set him up in the little sewing room. The nearby bathroom was for his convenience. Not a drink since the accident, his appeals all denied. Soon he was able to make his way downstairs, where he would sit staring around him with his plastered leg stretched out. He only vaguely resembled the drunken old bum, he was clean and shaved and had been given new clothes.

One day when Jack came home from work he found his lovely wife and his guest sitting on the couch, hands entwined and tears flowing down their cheeks. Thinking to entertain John she had brought out the family photo album. There on the first page, the faded picture of an older lady had caught his eye.

"Who is that lady." the old man asked? She replied, "That's Jack's Mom she died eleven years ago."

That brought the flow of anguished tears, as the old man realized the terrible suffering that he had caused her and his family.

Jamaican Evening Out

What a beautiful country and what a wonderful climate. What could be better than living where it's summer all year round? Here we are, the Trans Canada Airlines, North Star crew on a three-day layover. Back in the day, travelling by air took much longer than it does today. Our flight from Toronto to Kingston with a stop en route to Nassau and Montego Bay, took an exhausting ten hours. The flight left early the following morning and we remained on the Island until the return of the next flight. There were five crew-members on that airplane, the Captain, First Officer, Navigator, a Purser and a Stewardess.

Travelling by air is a lot different today, now huge jet-planes with hundreds of passengers, hurtle into the sky and at nearly six hundred miles an hour can operate the return trip without the need of the crew to lay over. Where-as the Douglas DC4 aka "North Star" with its four Merlin engines only carried 44 passengers plodding along at 225 mph, today's jets can carry up to 400 passengers at nearly 600 mph in quiet comfort. And the noise, well let's say things are a lot different today.

We stayed at the Morgan's Harbour Inn. Located on a spit on land just past the airport. Walking distance to the Fort Royal and the community of Port Royal. I stayed at that place several times and was always thrilled by my good fortune. Our rooms were en suite , air-conditioned and very comfortable. There was no swimming pool, rather a small bay beside which the motel was located, had been fenced off from the sea and the acre or so what remained was for the use of the guests.

At first we were reluctant to bathe there as a huge Barracuda was a permanent occupant of the area, it was quite small when it was trapped inside the swimming safety fence and as it had grown and matured it had to remain in semi captivity. Sandy, the barman, would lend us fishing rods, and we would bait our hooks with our breakfast bacon, But the four foot long fish , which we called Barry, remained free.

The ship "Sea Diver" was tied up to our hotel dock, and its crew led by Captain Weems USN ret'd, would join us at the bar where we would swap yarns. The Sea Diver was doing archeological research of the sunken city of the old Port Royal for several weeks and it was exciting to hear the crew relate their adventures.

The expedition was sponsored by a syndicate of three , the National Geographic magazine, the Government Of Jamaica and the owner of the Sea Diver, Mr Ed Link nb.. We watched the divers who would bring ashore a variety of relics and on one occasion several small brass cannons. Those were wonderful care-free days.

On several occasions I would go for a stroll to the old Fort and join a guided tour and it was a joy to hear the colorful guide telling the history of that wonderful place and time. The fort was built centuries ago in the form of a ship. Manned by British sailors would carry out its function as if it was a ship of the line. After the great earthquake which sunk the town of Port Royal, the fort was raised out of the sea and is now on dry land.

It was a surprise to find, on one of our trips, that the famous movie star, Errol Flynn, and a few of his friends, including actor Gig Young, had tied up their yacht at our Hotel Dock and were planning on an extended stay. They mixed freely with the guests and every day would use the swim area.

Errol was a great big handsome man and at that time I imagine was in his early fifties. He was suffering with serious back pain and spent most of the time on his yacht resting, but there was one occasion while we were at the bar he suggested we all go down to Kingston and have dinner at his favorite club, The Green Lantern, who could resist this offer. Later, approximately ten of us, ordered cabs and we were on our way into the capitol.

As we approached the Green Lantern we were met by the wonderful sound of the steel band playing some unusually lovely music. I can still imagine its thrill. We were found a huge table where we enjoyed a most pleasant evening of Rum, Curried Goat and rice, music and dancing. The club was a rough and tumble sort of a place and we gradually adopted the use of its more common name "The Green Latrine". After a couple of hours Errol begged off and took a cab back to the Morgans Harbour. We must have stayed until about ten, we were flying home tomorrow and must get our rest.

Now-a-days, most tourists visit the Montego Bay area where a lot of modern hotels have been built, and the beaches are of beautiful silver sand and where the sea is a panorama of gorgeous blues. But for me, the real Jamaica is Kingston and the Morgans Harbour when we were more innocent and the tourists who were the island's life's blood, were always welcomed with a smile and happy music.*

NB: Mr Ed Link, was the inventor of the Link Trainer, which was a device which helped pilots to learn to fly. Captain Van Weems was known in the flying community for having developed the navigational charts which were vital back in the old days.

Dinner at Dirty Dick's
(A Crew Layover)

Old Tom, the doorman of the Kensington Palace Hotel in London, was dressed in his working uniform of quasi-military elegance. It was complete with shiny medals and top-hat, and he informed me that a very nice place to go for lunch was Dirty Dick's pub, near the Underground Station at Liverpool Street. He had told me that the pub served typically British food from a huge buffet and that I wouldn't be disappointed. Just take the number nine bus and ask the conductor to let you off at Dirty Dick's.

There was a bus stop on High Street, just across the road from our hotel, and in no time at all a number nine bus came along. I had no difficulty in locating the pub, which from the outside looked not much different from any other. With the exception, as you approached, you could hear the buzz of friendly conversation interspersed with laughter and cheerful bonhomie. I would much rather have been with one or two friends as I preferred company in this type of situation. It was a bit of a surprise to me as I entered, to see the enormous buffet. It started and continued along the left side of the very large dining room.

On the right side of the room, resting on trestles, was a row of huge, oaken, barrels containing a variety of sweet, wines from Spain. I called them sherries as I later discovered, they were of the finest quality, aged in oak and emitted an aroma and taste not usually found in an ordinary pub. At the far end of the room were a few small tables and chairs but most of the large crowd of customers were enjoying their lunch standing at high, tiny, tables.

Many of the foods on offer would not be served at a buffet in Canada. Spread out on this twenty foot long counter were the usual boiled and baked hams where a server dressed in white coveralls would carve you your portion. Further along there were great joints of cold, roast beef, leg of pork, geese, turkey, capons and game. Next, were a selection of pies; veal and ham pie, steak and kidney, and pork pies in various flavors. There was an array of salads and pickles, piccalilli, pickled onions and chutneys like I had never seen before. The sea-food was typically British, great pans of jellied eels, smoked eels, winkles, cockles, clams, mussels, buttered shrimp, crab, lobster and others I couldn't recognize, all displayed on a table of crushed ice.

The luncheon crowds pressed up to the buffet, when served they passed along to the interior of the room. After paying for their meal, they found a free spot, ate their food all the while there was a loud hum of cheerful chatting and friendly banter. I sampled a little of everything from the huge selection and was pleasantly surprised at the modest price. I believe that was the finest meal I ever had, although the jellied eel was a bit too gross for my taste. In the line-up I had struck up a conversation with one of the locals and found myself at his table, enjoying my lunch. As he was leaving he said with a wink, "Have you had a drink at the downstairs bar?"

I was about to ask him for more details when he left with a smile on his face. I had finished my meal and as I was feeling a bit thirsty. I started for the narrow stairway which led to the lower level. The downstairs area was a long, narrow room with a bar at the far end. The ceiling and walls of the room were covered with folding money, as well as adorned with letters and postage stamps from every country in the world. I spent a few minutes looking at this amazing graffiti and discovered stamps, from tiny countries which I had never heard of; there was even a postcard from Tonga.

As I neared the bar my eyes were drawn to a board about two feet square beside the bar, on which was fastened the stretched and desiccated, snarling body of a dead, black cat. A small sign was attached which read "stroke the cat for luck."

There were other dried out small animals about the rafters of the ceiling, which appeared to be rats and mice. They had been there for a long time. I observed the barman in conversation with an unusually, attired black, man, nursing a scotch and soda in his hand. The customer was dressed in what in some circles might be thought of as posh, upper, middle, class, formal wear. His shoes were black patent with yellow spats; he wore black, pin-striped pants and a black city jacket; with a white, starched, shirt complete with an air-force, striped, tie. A furled umbrella over his arm and a bowler, topped off his outfit. One foot was resting on the brass bar-rail.

As I approached, the barman continued to encourage the black person to stroke the cat for luck, while he told the story of Dick, the tavern owner. As the story goes, in 1798, on the eve of his marriage to a beautiful, young, girl, he thought he had been jilted only to discover, to his horror, that his bride-to-be had died in a terrible accident and from that time on he had never washed or cleaned up his bar. He had also kept the bridal chamber exactly as it was, where a glorious banquet had been arranged to celebrate the nuptials. The cat, a symbol of bad luck if crossing your path at night, had crossed Dick's path so when he was at the height of his suffering, he viciously clubbed it to death and stretched its carcass as it appeared to this very day. As everybody knows, however, touching a "dead" black cat often brings astonishing good luck. It struck me at the time that Paddy, the bar-man, was a very persuasive storyteller.

The stranger may have been oddly dressed but he was no fool, and it took quite a while for Paddy to convince the customer to stroke the dead cat. The crowd in the pub had been listening to Paddy's line and sensing a laugh, had gathered closer to the bar. The smile on the man's face was a nervous one and now it was obvious that he must have wished he was somewhere else. He had reached the point where he could no longer vacillate and must be a good sport. What on earth harm could there be in touching a dead cat? Just a bag of bones, two hundred years old. He leaned forward to touch the cat, while at the same time the Irishman pressed a little switch beneath the bar. Suddenly the cat gave a leap from its rack and at the same time a fearful scream came out of the cat's jaws, followed in a split second by an agonized scream which came from the black man's throat. The man stared and I could swear he paled, but quickly gained composure. He joined in the general laughter of the crowd at the bar, most of whom had been caught by the dead cat trick, at one time or other.

Well, we ordered more drinks and still tittering realized that Paddy had more wisdom to dispense. "Yes Gentlemen," he said, and pointing to a small door in the wall. "Behind that wall is the bridal chamber, exactly as it was all those years ago, and if you want to have a look at that beautiful chamber it will cost you only one shilling, which will be donated to the RSPCA, earmarked for the cat division."

He continued to tell us more history of Dick and the London of the late eighteenth century. He kept us all entranced as he held our attention as only an Irish storyteller can. The little door in the wall looked more and more fascinating and after a while I found a shilling and deposited it on the counter.

I said "Here Paddy, I'll have a shilling's worth." Paddy took out the big brass key and unfastened the lock. I stood in front and opened the trap door, which flew open and on the shelf was an old, porcelain chamber pot, a thunder mug, a piss pot which was dirty and cracked and a sign which read "Don't tell the others."

I stared for a few minutes then muttering "very interesting," then proceeded to close the hatch. There was an immediate clamor from the others while they plunked down their shillings.

Post script:
The dead animals were, in fact, clever fakes which, in the subdued lighting, looked very real.

The Old Bailey
(Layover in London)

Some of my yarns are experiences I had with Purser, Tom Mills and when I read them they bring back pleasant memories. My, what wonderful people we knew in those days and I fondly recall the marvelous adventures we had.

I remember when Tom and I went to the Old Bailey in London to watch an attempted murder trial. We were allowed into the courtroom because "we were visiting attorneys from Canada." This was certainly not the case, so I had better explain the situation.

Tom and I, along with two of our colleagues, approached the entrance to courtroom number one. We were stopped by the policeman at the door of the court and asked for our identification. We had no suitable I.D. except for our airport passes. The four of us, wearing our uniform overcoats, were quite disappointed.

The officer seemed to be a friendly sort of chap, and asked us if we were attorneys visiting from Canada? We naturally replied that we were crew members on a layover in London. He asked us again if we were Canadian lawyers. Once again, we tried to explain that we worked for Trans Canada Airlines. The officer cut us short in our explanation and re-asserted that we were visiting lawyers. At the same time, Ruth Fox caught on to the subterfuge and along with our acceptance of our new status, we were permitted access to the courtroom.

This was all new to me as I've never been in a criminal court before. I was very impressed by the architecture and the heavy dark furniture. Nearly every seat was taken. There were a lot of people, mainly lawyers and prosecutors wearing funny, little white wigs, which seemed to be sitting on top of their heads rather than actually being worn. Most of the officers of the court were men. The judge was wearing long, black robes and wore a different, fuller and longer type of wig headpiece. It struck me that the differences in head wear may have had something to do with position or status.

Anyway, while the four of us were rubbernecking around, a loud voice called out "Hear Ye, Hear Ye," the court of the Queens' bench is now in session etc., or words to that effect. A panel of the defendant's peers sat in two tiers, in a secure area of the courtroom. I noticed, at the time that everyone, including the jury, looked guilty of something questionable.

The court proceedings began to unfold. Apparently, a group of young men and women had been at a house party, including the plaintiff and the defendant and their respective girlfriends. The party had progressed in the usual way, with refreshments and alcoholic beverages. Some time later in the evening the effects of the booze became apparent. The girls decided that it would be exciting to have some sort of relationship with the others' boyfriend.

There are all types of techniques of flirtatious behavior, to be displayed, some more subtle than others. The approach used in this instance was for the girl to quietly approach the other's friend and ask for a cigarette. Being out of cigarettes he asked the other group members for a fag and received one from the defendant. This information was extracted from the reluctant witness and it was difficult to follow as most of the language of the accused was spoken with a broad cockney accent. Several times his Lordship was obliged to ask for clarification of some cockney term.

Slowly, a picture of the party was built in the minds of the spectators. One had the impression of twenty to thirty young, working class people, crammed into a small council house.

Most parties consisted of blaring music, dancing, loud laughter and ribald talk. Jokes and innuendo were flying and some of the group were becoming more friendly than sensible under the circumstances. It appeared that the small kitchen in the house had held the food. Situated on the table was a bread-board, loaves of bread, sandwich fillings etc., and a long, sharp, kitchen knife were all laid out.

The girl needed a light for her smoke, but instead of smoking the two friends began to kiss each other. The defendant entered the kitchen to get some food just as his girl and his friend, the plaintiff, were in a close and compromising situation.

He shouted out, "Get your hands off my girl."

In return she called out, "I'm only having a cigarette."

Rather than believe her statement, he trusted his own eyes, and giving his friend a push separated the two would-be lovers. You must imagine these young people roused in sexual passion, at the same time not wishing to look a fool in the eyes of their lovers. Gradually, the angry shouting and cursing gave way to coarser invective and to more physical confrontation. The two young men, urged on by the two young women, faced each other a nose length apart in that tiny, crowded, kitchen, with the background music and laughter filling the house with noise.

"I thought to myself, as I listened to the circumstances of the event being drawn from the witnesses, that beyond any doubt the two men were guilty, without any question, of rank stupidity, if nothing else. However, of course the charge was not that of stupidity but of attempted murder."

The sordid details continued. The expression on his Lordships' face was showing his disgust. It soon became clear that the defendant, having received much the worse of the violence, made a final effort to re-assert himself. In desperation he had grabbed the kitchen knife and stabbed his friend in the chest. The knife had pierced the others chest and finally rested in the poor mans' heart. He fell to the floor and lay still. Blood began to ooze all over the kitchen floor.

Even though we were several hours in the courtroom listening to evidence being presented, that, in effect, was the basic facts of the matter.

Meanwhile, at the party the noise continued but the screaming in the kitchen was investigated. The blood-covered body was found lying on the floor, the girlfriend cradling his head in her arms and sobbing in grief and fear. One person more lucid than the others called for an ambulance which appeared within minutes and the victim was whisked away to the nearby hospital. The police arrived and arrested the suspect.

The stabbed man remained in hospital for five months. It was touch and go. Superb, professional, medical care saved the man's life. Now a year after the incident, the case was being heard.

The Lord Justice gave the jury its instructions.

He added the comment that "Having heard the full details of the case I find it difficult to determine from the evidence presented, as to who was the plaintiff and who was the defendant, they both looked equally guilty to me."

It didn't take the jury long to deliberate and find the defendant guilty as charged.

To Kill A Chicken

We lived in Caledon when the children were growing up. We had a wonderful life, but I regret to say I found the continuous work to be a hardship. All sorts of animals became members of our family and with each addition, however, well-intentioned, made more work for Kay, my wife and me. (I accept the blame for the cattle).

I decided that I would add to our menagerie several beef cattle. Herefords to be precise. Well known for being healthy and easily marketable. I was under the impression that there was a government subsidy that was also available. I looked into this and discovered like many government offerings, there were strings attached and this did not apply to "gentleman or hobby farmers." What a misnomer that was! We live and learn. Now, to get back to the chickens. We had horses, cows, ducks, two dogs, five kids and many other kinds of critters who just passed through. Including the neighbors dogs who caused us no end of trouble.

At the Caledon Central School, as well as at the regular school their subjects included classes on living animals. These were part of the curriculum. What a wonderful idea and how practical, for the majority of the students who lived on farms. Due to the gentle and caring nature of our children, they often got to bring the classroom animals home, when the lessons were over. Kay and I, always agreed to open our house and make the new family members welcome.

The fowl grew quickly and being "range raised" had free run of the property and dropped their waste all over the place. They may have been pretty birds but they were filthy creatures. Then one day twelve baby chicks arrived. Twelve, tiny bundles of cute, cheeping yellow fluff. And the children, with their eyes glowing with delight and smiles to match the sun shining in the blue sky, carrying those beautiful, little, God's creatures home. Of course we'll make room for them we agreed.

First we left the chicks in a warm, flat, box which we placed in the kitchen with a dish of fresh water. Then we were off to the feed store to buy fifty pounds of chicken-feed. How quickly those critters grew, and so did the smell and the noise. Within a week they had out-grown their kitchen accommodation and along with the nasty smell we re-located them to a place in Dutchie's stable. There the chickens with unlimited space and food, grew to be great, big, aggressive beasts.

Often they would show their dis-pleasure by attacking us, if we were a little slow in giving them their ration of grain. We had learned that the breed of those birds was Leghorns, and within a few months they had reached the height of about three feet, when stretched out tall on tip-toe. They were quite scary when several of these brutes would fly at you, with their short wings flapping and with shrill cries from their yellow, sharp, pointed bills. They were only chickens weren't they? Chickens can't harm you!

Chickens can't fly, that is true, but they can jump fences that are several feet high. What is meant by "free range hens?" Of course, it means they have out-smarted their keeper and have the run of the place. They can eat anything and fowl the pathways, if you'll pardon the pun. There was no way we would have these semi-wild chickens on our property when winter-time arrives. And it was when the days began to shorten and the evenings began to cool, that we decided the day of reckoning had arrived. Kay and the kids refused to have any part of this operation. So that left Kay's mom and me to be the butchers. By this time the chickens were about five pounds of muscle and feathers with crowing, sharp, beaks. They were fierce-looking and eyeing where they could see a weak spot in their victims' defenses.

Molly, Kay's Mom, had been brought up on a farm in Ireland, she knew what to do. She explained how you would hold the bird up by the feet, and let its head dangle, then give a sharp blow with the edge of your hand, just south of the head. We tried that method and had to agree that's a lie, it can't be done.

Perhaps Canadian chickens are smarter than their Irish brethren. When a chicken is held up by the feet, it has the habit of twisting its neck to be able to see forward, as this is a normal reaction. The arch of the neck, if held still over a block of wood and you should be ready with a swift chop with an axe. That would do the trick. I explained what I had in mind to Molly and gave her the axe.

The problem is that chickens are gifted with second sight and they won't cooperate. I took the axe while Molly held the bird, still we were not able to terminate it.

Then I had an idea, "Molly" I said, "Would you hold the brute while I get my gun?"

I ran to get my .22 rifle and loaded it with shorts.

"Hold still Molly, I'll shoot it in the head." I said, but this was easier said than done.

After several shots at the uncooperative creature we decided to call a halt to the exercise. We allowed the birds to go free and we went indoors for a cup of tea.

"Soon the kids will be home from school and we don't want them to see what we are doing," she said. "We'll try again tomorrow."

The following day I called the Caledon East Butcher and explained our problem. He told us about his new service, of preparing live birds for the freezer, at five dollars each.

It took us a couple of hours to round up the flock of chickens and bag them, then off to the butchers. Problem solved, I couldn't help smiling with relief. The entire operation cost us sixty dollars. And we ended the transaction with a freezer full, of frozen chickens. It must have been about a year later that we finally disposed of those birds. We couldn't bring ourselves to eat them. And I bet you couldn't either.

The Trouble With Mice

In a million years you would never believe all the trouble Luigi took to keep his bakery clean and free from vermin. He even went as far as to bag every loaf of his bread, pies and cakes to keep the flies away.

I don't think anyone would doubt the integrity of that fine gentleman, who had produced the finest baked goods for more than twenty years. It is one thing to satisfy the customer that the baked goods are the finest, freshest and tastiest possible. As for the extra penny or two which was paid as a premium for such fine products, was worth it. On the other hand there are health regulations to contend with.

Now it came to pass that in the year 2008, there was a push in our city for the Public Health Inspectors to closely examine our bakeries and restaurants. It appeared there had been a number of complaints from customers to the effect that they had seen mouse droppings in a restaurant, or claimed that they had become ill, as a result of bad food. We have all heard about certain ethnic restaurants, where the proprietors may be a little lax, in keeping their premises up to the rigid standards required of the Government Health Services. Sometimes these complaints may be valid.

Everyone must be aware that the warmth of the ovens and the products prepared by your local baker, are the two basic needs of a number of small animals. Put a male and a female mouse in the average bakery, unchecked, and I guarantee there will be a serious infestation in a very short space of time.

Controlling the mouse population is easy you might believe, but don't forget how the government controls all our efforts, in every walk of life. The two easiest devices to ensure a minimum population of mice are trapping, (baiting with Warfarin rat-poison) and the mouse's natural enemy, the kitty cat. In its wisdom the authorities have declared that these tools may not be used.

Swabbing floors of the bakery with a strong disinfectant is recommended, but I promise you, this will not rid you of mice, however, you will kill various types of bacteria. So since the mice are very persistent as well as being un-cooperative, the baker must resort to the old stand-by, the spring-loaded trap. Mice may be disgusting creatures but they are not stupid, and it does not take these creatures long to learn to avoid traps, no matter how tasty the bait may be. So now all the regular methods of eliminating mice are not to be used, and the inspectors are coming!

But every cloud has a silver lining. Luigi had a nine-year-old daughter who was very smart and loved animals. The little girl, Maria, had been one of the teacher's favorites since she was in kindergarten. Maria had always shown herself to be serious and responsible. She would be rewarded for her diligence, by helping the teacher with some of her chores, like collecting work-books and wiping the black-board, were two of her favorites.

So when the time came for the teacher to give classes in biology she brought a number of small animals into the class-room. Maria, being the teacher's pet, got to feed them.

Soon the day-old chicks were dispensed with and the puppy went back to the pound, all that was left was the little mouse and the snake. Well, mice are a favorite food of the snake. Yes, you guessed it, mistakes happen and due to an unfortunate upset, the snake enjoyed an extra and unexpected meal. Well, no problem, there are lots of mice and that school mouse could easily be replaced.

What's that got to do with the price of cheese? Well, coincidently with that occurrence, Luigi was at school at a P.T.A. meeting, when this story was told to the doting Dad.

He began to smile to himself realizing that his troubles at work were over. He would get a snake and let it run free in the bakery. A snake that size would have no trouble, it could follow a mouse and have no trouble swallowing it whole, no muss, no fuss, no noise and no need to feed the brute. Also, no hair and no allergies. What a perfect mouser. Not only that but he would buy a large quantity of snakes and rent them out to other bakeries, who experienced the same problem. He could possibly make a fortune which is impossible to do, in the baking trade.

Three weeks later the inspectors made their unexpected visit to the bakery. Following a thorough examination of the premises, Luigi's Bakery was presented with a "Gold Star" rating for excellence. This was posted with pride near the front door, for everyone to see. Since that time there hasn't been a trace of a mouse.

However, his wife has left him. Oh yes, the mice have disappeared but she refuses to live in the upstairs apartment with a wild snake on the loose in the main floor bakery. Our hero, with his great success, has no plans to find someone to get rid of his snake. His greatest problem is keeping the smile off his face.

Cat Trouble

A lot of people dote on their pet, and that's all right as sometimes they get more love and affection from their cat or dog than ever they would receive from a fellow human being. Why, earlier on the news today I heard that a dog was left a hundred million dollars by his late owner, and let's admit it, that is an awful lot of love. I personally do not understand why anyone is actually able to love a cat. A cat always seems unable to express affection. Seems they are always able to demand attention and care. People do love cats, just because I don't understand that, doesn't make it wrong.

The airline I used to work for makes a lot of money carrying pets from one place to another. Special arrangements are made to satisfy a customer's needs, when caring for the traveling pet. There are ways to get special dispensation and allow certain animals to travel in the passenger cabin, but that does not happen often.

A working dog has the legal right to travel with its owner, in the cabin when flying. In that situation it does not need to be caged. A special area in the aircraft cargo hold is reserved for the animal passengers, air-conditioned and pressurized. The animal must be caged and it is often, for obvious reasons, sedated so it will not be stressed by the strange environment.

The Flight Attendant is alerted that an animal is on board and can re-assure the owner that his or her pet is comfortable. The ramp personnel go out of their way to give the traveling pet all the appropriate tender love and care (TLC).

When there is an interruption in the flight, there is always a kindly soul to provide the pet with fresh water and in some cases even exercise the pet. Yes, my company goes to extreme lengths to satisfy the customer. During my career of thirty-five years with the airline, I have had a lot of experience with traveling animals. I've cared for dogs and cats on many occasions but also monkeys, swans, snakes, macaws and even horses and prize cattle. On one occasion half a million day-old chicks were on a 747 flight to Egypt.

Sadly, all handling of this special cargo is not successful. I have often wondered if a pet were to die en-route, would the customer get the fare refunded? In the case of a human passenger dying in flight, I know for a fact that they don't get their money back. We certainly never guarantee "Arrive Alive," as a slogan.

Come to think about it, I wonder if I would be the recipient of an employee award if I make the suggestion, what a great slogan that would be. Well, as often happens when chatting with fellow airline, re-tired employees at our monthly coffee klatch, stories are told that make you laugh, or cry, or wonder. My friend Bob, who always has a tale to tell, once again brought on a fit of laughter when he told the tale of the dead cat.

When flight 148 arrived from Vancouver that day, Jan, the big Dutch-man went out to the airplane to bring the cat into the baggage area in preparation for its delivery to the customer. The cat box was carefully transported to our office. Since there was no movement in the box, we carefully opened it and there to our dismay, we found the cat was dead, stiff as a board.

Well, Jan had been involved with a dead animal on a previous occasion and had no intention of going through that kind of investigation again. He sensibly thought that there can't be a lot of difference between cats. As there were several cats running about the place keeping down the mice, he would catch one. Of course it should resemble the dead cat and he would replace it, and everybody should be happy.

A phone call was made to the person living in Toronto to whom the cat was addressed. They informed her that her cat had arrived from Vancouver and was at the baggage office ready to be picked up.

In the meantime, Jan and several of the office staff were on the hunt around the building for a replacement for the dead Tabby. Well, sure enough a friendly cat, the image of the dead Tabby, was located. The animal was put in the travelling cat-box, on the counter waiting to be collected. Everyone went about their work, satisfied they had solved a serious problem for the company. Jan even was the recipient of a pat on the back for his resourcefulness.

Well, it was an hour or so later that the customer arrived to collect her cat.

When it was handed over to her and when she saw the live cat, she screamed…"that's not my cat, my cat is dead, it was sent here so I could have it stuffed."

Only with the best of good fortune, was Jan able to retrieve the dead cat from the trash bin and carefully carry it to its owner, who accepted the explanations in good humor.

Crawford Lake
Provincial Park, Ontario

In the early eighties I was part of a small team of budding archeologists who spent two exciting summers, digging at the Crawford Lake Indian Village site. There were twelve of us, and our leader was William Finlayson, PhD., who was at that time also the curator of the Museum of Indian Archeology in London, Ontario. This particular site was identified as having been populated, several hundred years ago by a group of people of the Iroquois Nation. They apparently lived and farmed nearby.

Core samples of the lake bottom had been taken and subsequent studies had found a variety of pollens in the samples. These were dated and believed to have been deposited during the sixteenth century. The corn, squash and beans pollens which were identified, are known to be carried away from the source by air movements. These pollens would have been deposited in a natural way, within half of a mile distance. It was decided that as a result of this information a project would be created, under the auspices of the University of Toronto department of Archeology. Doctor Finlayson would be its leader.

Just to the north of Crawford Lake, a fairly level area was seen as the probable site of a village. Tests were conducted which confirmed this. Topsoil was removed and "Post Molds" were discovered, which indicated human activity. Dating of the post molds and the pollens confirmed the period of occupation. Our job entailed excavating and recording any artifacts we were able to discover.

I first met Dr. Finlayson at the site, where he, along with his wife and the rest of our group, walked over the property. It would be decided where exactly he would establish the reference point. We were all in a friendly and relaxed mood and walked the site together. We introduced ourselves and after a short time we seemed to gravitate toward those who seemed to be the most compatible. Small, informal groups were formed which soon meant we would be working together, as friends. I remember at the time, that our group included one young woman who was an Aboriginal person from a northern community. She was earning her degree at the University of Toronto.

It struck me at the time how seldom we see Native Canadians involved in Indian studies. This being the first and only "First Nations" person I had met in my three years involvement in this work.

The Datum Point was decided upon and registered and grids were laid out. These grids were five meter squares and divided into twenty five sections of one meter each. Each student was assigned two sections and instructed how to excavate. Our tools were simple, following the removal of any brush and sod, the rest of the work was done using a five inch trowel and a two gallon bucket to carry away the detritus.

It was hard work and though it was a beautiful, late spring day with a pleasant breeze, the work made us tired and sweaty. At about one o' clock we decided to drive to the nearby village of Campbellville, for lunch. Several members of our group found a comfortable spot in the shade and decided to rest for their lunch hour.

We returned around two o'clock and spent an enjoyable afternoon on our knees in our square. We only rested our tired backs while Doctor Finlayson gave a lecture on the know-how and where-fores of "Post Molds."

This was a subject in which he is an authority. Briefly, when a longhouse is being constructed the builder selects suitable, slender, flexible trees which form the skeleton of the house. Trees, which serve as poles are cut down, trimmed and inserted into a prepared hole, two or three feet deep.

The poles are placed to form the perimeter of the building, about three feet apart. The tops of the poles are bent over and attached to their opposite member, which forms the roof. Smaller branches interlace this foundation. Spaces are left in the roof to allow smoke, from the fires to escape. Birch bark covers the long-house to keep it weatherproof. There are skins at the doors to allow entry for up to forty occupants.

After ten to twenty years the poles rot at their base and the house is no longer habitable and is re-built on fresh ground. Eventually, the base of the poles rot away and it is the mold that is left which later enquirers find of use in their studies. The post molds are easily discernible as the process stains the earth in its immediate vicinity.

We novices, under the supervision of Doctor Bill Finlayson, soon became adept at the digging technique. In our assigned squares we were able to scrape away the soil in shallow layers, using the sides of our trowels. We were shown how to identify the shards of pottery and each fragment was put in a plastic envelope, with its exact location and depth recorded.

Sometimes we would dig for hours before something of interest was found, and when we unearthed a find we would holler for joy and boast of our discovery. Often, our enthusiasm would be dampened when the gem we found turned out to be a small stone. However, sufficient, interesting, items were found and identified which helped to maintain our enthusiasm.

An excited scream came from Marian, in the next square to mine when she unearthed something very special. It was a complete pot. Dr. Finlayson took over the responsibility of this important find. He removed the entire piece of ground to his lab, for more careful study. Later, he explained that the pot may have contained the remains of what was being prepared for a meal. The molecules of the remains would be more accurately identified, under a more controlled atmosphere.

I thought the few bits and pieces we found were hardly worth the effort. However, it is surprising how the experienced scholar can read such detail, from so little evidence. A few shards of pottery, a few broken tools, some bones and some preserved organic remains. Those items may yield the history of the First Nations people who lived in villages many years ago.

I found a small piece of a clay pipe and you would have thought I had unearthed a gold watch, judging by the excitement that discovery had caused.

Today, the Indian village has been re-constructed in much of its original form and is open to the public, for a few dollars entrance fee. You can walk that space and gain a sense how the earlier inhabitants passed their days at work or play. If you are fortunate enough to possess a vivid imagination put it to good use. Add more to the unspoken story of those long-gone folks. They were human beings very much like us, whose main interest, like ourselves, was to do their daily work to wrest a living from their environment.

I was the oldest of the students and found myself paired with the youngest, on several assignments. My team-mate's name was Harold and he was nineteen, at that time. We were sent to the village, to purchase the materials to make a sieve, to filter out our diggings.

To ensure that we wouldn't let anything escape our notice. Harold mentioned to me that the other young male student was derisive of our enthusiasm, and he was only attending the course to pick up an easy credit. He was studying to be a medical doctor and this course was a breeze for him.

Most of us had to study and work hard at the course to obtain a satisfactory mark. The superior attitude of our friend, we found quite disconcerting. Harold thought it might be a good idea to slip into the Kresge's Store and have a look around. We purchased the wire and wood for our sieve and Harold disappeared for a few minutes. We paid for our supplies and Harold paid the thirty five cents for his purchase.

Later, he explained that he had bought some glass beads. At the end of the day he would spike our future doctor's square with those beads, for a gag, to get a laugh. This plan was to take our friend down a peg or two when the beads were found in our dig. Well, the following morning, shortly after we started digging, our friend gave a loud, excited, yell as he came across the first of the "artifacts."

We gathered around and congratulated our friend, who was preening himself for his cleverness. Harold and I were chuckling quietly to ourselves, all the while. This performance repeated itself several times as more beads were unearthed and we had a few laughs, at his expense. Mind you when the truth was out, he took it all very well and so did the Instructor, and we all enjoyed the trick we played.

We got to know another person who was a Tutorial Assistant in the department of Archeology at the University of Toronto. Deborah Berg was a very pleasant young woman who was working on her PhD. Debbie's unusual specialty was preparing the skeletons of dead animals and she gave us a lecture on the subject. She would receive small, dead animals from all over the world. She would seal the bodies in a glass container with selected insects, until only the bones remained. As a career it was definitely a unique choice. Although none of our group appeared to be interested in pursuing that type of career.

If you visit a location in the Town of Milton, Ontario, on Steeles Avenue West, east of Guelph Line, at the Crawford Lake Conservation area you can tour the re-established Indian village. This is a diorama depicting the lifestyle of the First Nation's people who lived there prior to the arrival of the Europeans. This is a wonderful historical site.

The Lady Firefighter

I don't expect you to believe this little tale, after all it has been said that truth can often be stranger than fiction. I realize that I have had some experiences which I find hard to believe even though I was there. However, let me explain that odd meeting with that fire-fighter, who hailed from the State of New York, the home of heroes, in a small town just a few miles out of Albany.

I was travelling on the New York Freeway heading east. I was en route to Syracuse to attend the Fall Antiques Auction. It was a pleasant September evening and I was on my own. It was so relaxing listening to the radio, the sun was behind me and the traffic was light. I had left my home in Niagara Falls early in the morning. I had been driving for several hours and I needed a rest and a meal. I pulled off the highway and stopped at the booth to pay my toll. I recall the cost in those days was something like two or three cents per mile.

The booth operator was a pleasant-spoken man, and told me to try to keep clear of the next small town, I believe it was called Upton, N.Y., as there had been a nasty fire and the traffic was being detoured, I thanked the man and waved good-bye.

Within fifteen minutes there was a sign on the roadside encouraging me to come in for food. The sign was lit with neon and simply said "EATS home cookin."

I parked in the handicap spot near the entrance and went in the roadside cafe. There were a lot of people in the restaurant, but I found a seat and the waitress came over, her name-tag telling the world that she was "Maria." Like majority of New Yorkers I have met, she was friendly, a tad brash, and a darn good-looker. Maria gave me a cheerful smile and handed me the menu.

I gave my order and took off to the washroom. When I returned to my table, over there in the corner, I noticed there was a woman sitting in the opposite chair. She nodded her greeting and inclined her head and she asked, "Do you mind if I join you?"

"No, I'd like the company" I replied, adding with a smile "My name's Trev."

The lady was about thirty, and looked ever so tired and sad. She was wearing some type of uniform and she smelled of smoke. It was her eyes that mostly caught my attention, deep-set and grey, dark shadowed and lined and oh, looking so world weary. I thought to myself that here was a lady who had seen profound pain. The server seemed run off her feet yet still able to appear unflustered. Soon she brought my meal and wished me "Bon Appetite," as I started to eat.

I noticed the lady just sat there, with no food in front of her, however, she seemed to want to talk. "The food is good." I said by way of an opener. "Can I get you something?" She shook her head "No," then she seemed to become more animated and told me that she had been working on putting out the fire nearby. She had just come in for a few minutes to rest. Then it struck me, the uniform and the smell of smoke, I realized that this young woman was a Fire-Fighter.

She leaned her exhausted body over the table and told me "This has been a horrible day, it wasn't my fault, I did everything that I could."

I noticed the strain in her voice, I just knew she had to share her thoughts. I put down my fork. "Would you like to tell me about it?" I asked. She seemed to gather her thoughts. Then in a hushed voice she said, "I was assigned to team number two and the six of us were fighting the fire in the nursery. The flames had taken hold and now it was a case of finding the kids who were not accounted for. I was on the second floor with my partner and the water from the fire-hose enabled me to continue my search. God, it was hot and the smoke and heat made it impossible to breathe without my air-pack."

She started to cough and I waited for her to continue. She was staring at my face but I knew she wasn't seeing me, she was seeing past me reliving the horror she must have recently been through.

"I could hear the muffled screams as I ran from room to room, everything was so confusing, the heat, the smoke, the danger, and I knew that any minute the floor was going to collapse."

"The chief had given the order to clear the building." She took a tissue from her pocket and dabbed at her eyes. "I could still hear that horrible, painful screaming, but now it was mixed with choking sobs. The last call came over my radio."

"Get out now," The chief yelled.

"My partner had already left, I was alone and frightened. Only the crackling sounds of the burning building could be heard and the crying had stopped. I couldn't leave the flaming ward until I had found the crying child, could I? I burst into the last room on the left and saw something swaddled in covers partway under the bed. In a panic I bent and scooped up the bundle, and found I was holding the limp body of a small, fair-haired child. Holding the child close to my chest I ran to the end of the corridor, just as the roof finally fell in and we were engulfed in flaming debris."

"I fought like a mad-woman to get out of that hell-hole, then with the child close to my chest I burst out of the flaming hell into the light and fell exhausted in the fresh air with that little girl clutched to my chest." She closed her eyes and I saw hot tears slide down her ashen cheeks. The next thing I remember I was sitting in the ambulance with an oxygen mask on my face, I asked the medic about the little girl."

"Sorry," he said, "She didn't make it."

"I was stunned with grief. As soon as I was able I got out of the ambulance and came in here."

With that she laid her head on the table and a long terrible sigh came from the poor woman's throat. I got out of my chair and dashed to find Maria to help her. She was busy serving some new customers.

"Maria," I called, "Please come here."

"More coffee?" She asked with a smile.

"No, no, please come and help me with the lady at my table."

She looked over to where I had been sitting, I followed her eyes. There was no-one at the table, all that was there was my half-eaten meal and my overcoat draped over the chair.

"I didn't see anyon,e" Maria said, "You must have been mistaken."

I paid my bill and left the cafe and overheard two men in conversation talking about the fire and the tragic loss of a young, woman fire-fighter who had died trying to save a child. I went back inside and searched the restaurant, she was nowhere to be found.